WILD OCEAN

TYSON WILD BOOK ONE

TRIPP ELLIS

WELCOME

Want more books like this?

You'll probably never hear about my new releases unless you join my newsletter.

SIGN UP HERE

1

The names and locations have been fictionalized to protect the innocent and the guilty.

The first time I died was nothing like I expected. There was no warm, soothing light. No chorus of angels. Nothing remotely comforting. There was only darkness. And the terrible sensation of falling.

With my stomach in my throat, I plummeted into the inky blackness. I had no illusions about where I was headed. With every inch I fell, the temperature grew hotter. The burning heat seared my skin, causing it to blister. The putrid stench of burnt flesh filled my nostrils. Pain engulfed my body. Throbbing and raw.

No, this wasn't a nightmare.

It was much, much worse.

Look, I was no saint. But I didn't think I was _that_ bad. In the back of my mind, I always knew I would have some explaining to do. But, up until this point, I had always been able to talk my way out of just about anything. I figured with a little creative persuasion, the Arbiter of Righteousness would say, "Hey, everybody makes mistakes. Come on in."

The pearly gates would open and it would be all clouds and angels. Angels that looked like they stepped out of a Victoria's Secret ad. At least, that would be my version of heaven.

That wasn't the case.

I wasn't even granted an audience with the Big Guy.

Nope.

It was straight to hell.

Every inch of my skin sent pain impulses to my brain. Not that I had a physical form anymore, I was just a spirit at this point. A lost soul. But it felt like I had a physical body, nonetheless. And it was being tortured.

If the fall was this bad, I couldn't imagine how horrible it was going to be once I reached my final destination.

Or maybe *this* was it?

Maybe I was doomed to fall through the darkness as my flesh melted from my bones for all eternity, repeating the process over and over again?

To be honest, I never much believed in heaven or hell. I figured maybe there's something out there beyond the plane of mortal existence. But mostly, I figured I'd be taking a long dirt nap after my final breath.

If this was my fate, it sucked. And sucked hard.

I started to panic. And I really wasn't prone to such a thing. I had always remained calm, cool, and collected. It was a requirement in my line of work.

A million thoughts raced through my mind. I wondered what the specific event was that sealed my fate?

It could have been any number of things.

Perhaps, it was an accumulation of multiple transgressions over my lifetime? Who knows? I wasn't sure I would ever find out. And maybe that was part of the torture—to spend an eternity in hell not knowing what you had done to deserve your fate.

I lost all sense of time. I could have been falling for seconds, minutes, hours, or days.

Then I felt a jolt to my chest. An electrical charge raced through my body. I felt my heart pump, and I saw a brilliant white light.

My chest sucked in a breath of air, and my eyes adjusted to the blinding light. I was flat on my back in the ER, staring at the light on the ceiling. The blip of my heartbeat pulsed on a nearby monitor. Doctors and nurses in teal green scrubs hovered over me, wearing face masks and wielding surgical implements.

"We've got him back," a nurse said in Spanish. "He's stabilizing."

The clear mask over my nose and mouth pumped in oxygen. I watched the medical team frantically try to save me. I felt detached, like it was happening to someone else. My eyes flicked to the bedside monitor, and I watched the craggy peaks and valleys of my heart climb up and down.

My blood pressure and my oxygen saturation were low. I heard one of them say something to the effect that, "It was a miracle I was alive."

I wasn't so sure about that. Judging by my near-death experience, I was pretty sure there wasn't anyone doing any miracles for me.

I couldn't tell if I was really conscious, or if I was watching this from outside myself, still somewhere in between *here* and *there*.

It was touch and go for a while. I wasn't sure if I had been only granted a temporary reprieve or if I was actually going to get a second chance? I probably didn't deserve one, but I would take it.

I didn't know what happened or how I got into this mess in the first place. But I knew one thing for certain—I never wanted to go back to hell. And I would do damn near anything to change my fate.

I wanted to believe it was just a crazy dream. I woke up in an intermediate care unit. The first thing I noticed was the cold steel of a handcuff around my left wrist, chained to the bed rail.

What the hell?

Things had gone seriously wrong.

My hands were covered in black ink. They had fingerprinted me while I was out. I was wearing one of those seafoam green gowns with little snowflake patterns repeating across the fabric. The kind of gown that you could never really tie properly and always left your ass half exposed.

They had pumped me full of the good drugs, but it didn't touch the pain in my chest. This wasn't the first time I had been shot.

The walls were painted in a pale institutional green, and the overhead florescent lights bathed the room in a sickly glow that made even the healthy nurses look ill.

The room was clean, but well-worn. Paint was chipped from the walls in places, and high-traffic areas had a coat of grime over them. The monitoring equipment looked like it had been there since the early '90s. This wasn't a state-of-the-art facility, and I began to wonder how clean those surgical instruments were in the ER. I didn't want to survive a gunshot wound to the chest only to die of sepsis a week later.

The nurse noticed my eyes were open. She looked fuzzy to me as she set a glass of water on the tray next to the bed. Everything was still a bit hazy. She held her thumb and index finger about an inch apart, "This much farther and you'd be dead, the doctor said."

I was fluent in Spanish and replied in kind, "Just lucky, I guess."

I flashed the best smile I could muster, but even that hurt. Just pushing enough air through my lungs to speak brought on stabbing pain.

The only thing that saved me was the carbon nanotube soft armor that I wore under my suit. It was lightweight IIIa armor effective up to .45-caliber rounds. Getting shot in real life is nothing like the movies. Even with soft armor, taking a bullet to the chest is like getting hit full swing with a base-ball bat. The impact causes a substantial deformation in the skin. You've seen the welts people suffer from paintball hits? Imagine that times 1,000. The impact is enough to spin you around, knock you off your feet, empty the air from your lungs, and sometimes stop your heart. To make matters worse, the bullet had pierced the back of the soft-armor.

That's where I got lucky. Sort of.

The armor had absorbed the brunt of the impact, so the velocity of the bullet was greatly reduced. It entered my upper chest, narrowly missing my subclavian artery and my brachial plexus. If the artery would have been nicked, I'd have bled out on the spot. The brachial plexus is a nerve bundle in your shoulder that controls motor function to your arm. Getting shot in the shoulder isn't as benign as it seems on TV.

The bullet was lodged in the muscle tissue of my pectoralis minor. The thoracic cavity wasn't penetrated. My brush with death was more a result of a drop in BP and my heart stopping while in surgery. I wasn't in a Level I trauma center, though I'm sure this place had no shortage of experience with gunshot wounds. The standard procedure was to remove the projectile and any other debris, debride the damaged tissue and remove surface contaminants, evaluate and repair neurovascular structures, and start IV antibiotics.

My chest and shoulder were multiple shades of purple, blue, green and red.

The nurse held the glass of water in front of my mouth and angled the straw toward my lips. It was one of those cocktail straws that you needed an industrial vacuum just to suck a few drops through. Needless to say, I didn't have any sucking power in my lungs.

She leaned in and whispered in broken English, "You in big trouble. *La policia esta' aqui para ti'.* What did you do?"

I shrugged, which again caused me to wince. I was going to have to stop doing that.

She pulled the cup away and set it down on the tray again.

I had no recollection of the last few days. Maybe the last few weeks. My brain was gummed up and I couldn't think clearly. There was a big hole in my memory.

I was hoping the man that stepped into my room would be able to fill some of the gaps. Though, he was probably looking for the same thing from me.

Answers.

He looked to be in his mid-50s, thinning hair on top with salt-and-pepper gray on the sides. His face was tanned and lined, and he had a large bulbous nose and a thin, trimmed mustache. He introduced himself as an investigative agent with the *Policía Federal Ministerial*. It was the Mexican version of the FBI. Their main focus was fighting corruption and organized crime.

Agent Gutierrez was his name. He wore a suit that was rumpled and worn and certainly didn't come from Brooks Brothers. He asked if I spoke Spanish and I nodded. With a smug grin he said the same thing the nurse had said. "You're in big trouble."

He towered above me, hovering over the railing. As he leaned in, his coat open slightly, revealing a patent leather shoulder holster. The once shiny surface was scuffed and worn. My eyes fell upon his Glock 9mm.

It was within reach.

A quick man could snatch it. But I was no longer a quick man. I was a fuzzy, groggy man that couldn't take a deep breath without eliciting pain.

The agent's eyes burned with anger, but he restrained himself, for the moment.

"What am I accused of?" I asked.

His lip curled up and quivered. If there weren't medical personnel in the room, he likely would have beaten me. "As if you don't know."

"I'm a little foggy on the details."

I could tell he thought I was playing a game with him, and he didn't like it one bit. Trying to contain his anger was a losing battle, and his pleasant facade was beginning to crack. "Three of my agents, along with a federal witness, are dead. Good men. Men with families. You killed them."

I said nothing.

His statement didn't jog my memory. It was still a big dark hole, like it had been redacted with a sharpie.

I couldn't absolutely say that I hadn't done it.

I had killed plenty of people before. Assassinations were my bag. And this sounded like a professional hit. But I couldn't put the *why* of it together. What was I doing in Mexico, taking out a witness? It just didn't make sense.

In my business, not everything is black and white. Most of it is varying shades of gray. Sometimes you have to do things of questionable moral value for the greater good. At least that's what you tell yourself.

That's what *they* tell you.

They are always trying to justify seemingly unjustifiable actions, but none of that is ever supposed to be *your* business. You are hired to do a job and not ask questions. Trust in the people above you. But the longer you are in this business, the harder that trust becomes. And you never really know who *they* actually are.

You do what you're told, like a good little soldier. Then you wake up one day, near death, realizing your life has gone horribly wrong, and you decide you don't want to be a good little soldier anymore.

3

"Who was the witness that I allegedly murdered?" I asked.

"Who are you working for?" Gutierrez replied. He pondered this for a moment. "The CIA, perhaps?"

"Not me. I'm just a civilian."

"Then tell me, civilian, what are you doing here?"

"Enjoying the sun and fun."

"Let me spell this out for you, and I will speak in English so I know you will understand. I don't think you are fully aware of the magnitude of the situation."

He was about to explain further when I heard the sound of suppressed fire in the hallway. The muffled bullets zipped down the corridor and slammed into the two agents standing guard outside the room. Blood erupted from their chests and they flopped to the ground.

Gutierrez turned his head toward the door and reached for his gun. Before he could grasp it, an assassin put two bullets into his chest. Crimson blood spewed from the wounds, staining my lovely green gown.

My heart pounded and adrenaline coursed through my veins. I didn't feel any pain as I reached for Gutierrez's weapon. My hand wrapped around the grip and yanked it from the holster as the agent's body fell across my bed.

It was the only thing that saved me.

His body absorbed several bullets that were meant for me. It gave me enough time to return fire.

Muzzle flash flickered from the barrel, and the sharp smell of gunpowder filled my nostrils. I squeezed off several rounds. Brass shell casings pinged against the floor. Smoke and haze filled the air, and the deafening bang filled my ears. The assassin hit the floor, and his gun clattered against the tile. Another man followed behind him and met the same fate.

Panicked screams of the hospital staff filtered down the corridor. A high-pitched whine filled my ears, but my hearing was slowly coming back to me. The blip of my heartbeat on the monitor raced. I dug into Gutierrez's pocket and fished out his keys. They clinked and chimed as I fumbled for the key to the handcuffs. Within moments, my wrist was free. It was more difficult to get the guardrail down on the bed than it was to get out of the handcuffs.

I snatched Gutierrez's wallet from his back pocket. It had a few thousand pesos, and more importantly, his federal identification. We looked nothing alike, but a quick flash might fool someone. I figured it might come in handy.

Gutierrez's body fell to the ground as I dropped the bed railing. I pulled the IV from my arm and climbed out of bed. The rush of adrenaline was wearing off, and the pain in my chest was excruciating. It felt like someone had stuck a red hot poker into my thoracic cavity.

I stumbled into the hallway. Staff hid in patient rooms and behind the counter at the nurses' station. They didn't care what I had done, and no one was getting paid enough to stop me. I ambled down the hallway, my ass hanging out the back of the gown. I must have looked ridiculous. Or crazed. Or both.

I found a pair of scrubs and a lab coat in the storage closet and pulled them on as quickly as possible. Talk about pain. The mere act of getting dressed hurt like hell. Fortunately I hadn't opened my stitches. But there was always the possibility of internal bleeding.

I slipped the 9mm into the pocket of the lab coat and took the elevator to the lobby and walked out of the building as if nothing happened. At the sidewalk, I flagged down a cab and slipped into the back seat, wearing non-skid hospital socks. Without hesitation, I gave the driver an address. It was like muscle memory. Words rolled off my tongue without a second thought. I didn't know what city I was in, but somehow I knew where I was staying.

I looked back through the rear window, looking to see if anyone followed. The hospital grew tiny and became a distant memory. Blood was already spotting my green shirt.

The cabdriver asked if I was a doctor.

I nodded my head.

We sped south on Rodrigo Gomez Avenue, then east on Xcaret, which wound around to Kukulcan. It didn't take me long to realize where I was—Cancun. I watched the glimmering teal water crash against white sand beaches as we headed to the resort area. There was no better cover than a tourist.

In the last few years, organized crime and violence has skyrocketed in the lush resort. The American government has even issued a travel advisory. The violence rarely happens in the tourist areas, but now and then a body is found on the beach or a back alley. It's usually taken care of quickly without much fanfare. That kind of thing is not good for business.

Acapulco used to be the playground of the rich and famous. Now it's the murder capital of Mexico. The east coast may face a similar fate if the tourists get scared away. It's getting to the point where it's almost impossible to operate a business without paying the cartels for the privilege. Cross the cartels and they will make a public demonstration of you. It's not uncommon to see their victims carved into multiple pieces and left in a public space with a warning message.

At my hotel, I played *dumb-drunk-tourist* and pretended I had lost my key card. I had another one within minutes and was directed to my room. Things were starting to come back to me in bits and pieces. The hotel looked familiar, and so did the room.

Despite having left a do not disturb sign on the door, the maid had refreshed the room. The curtains were wide open, and the tropical sun blasted into the room. The balcony offered a stunning view of the crystal waters. I moved to the sliding glass door and pulled the blackout curtains shut. Then I moved to the safe and punched in my pin code.

It's the same pin code I always use. I know, bad spy-craft, but it comes in handy in situations where your memory is a bit dodgy. I pulled out a small black travel wallet that fastened around the waist. Functional, but also very touristy. I unzipped the tear-resistant nylon and dug through the contents of the bag. It was filled with cash—both dollars and pesos. There were multiple passports with different cover IDs and a Bösch-Hauer PPQ-X2 9mm. It's one of the finest polymer, striker fired handguns available. Light and compact. It has one of the smoothest triggers, and a short reset that makes rapid firing a dream. It was my preferred handgun.

There were a few burner phones in the bag. It was time to call my handler and find out what the hell was going on.

4

"Start explaining," Isabella said in a sharp tone. Her angry voice filtered through the cell phone speaker, piercing my ear.

It was never a good idea to get on her bad side. She was a capable woman with immense resources. She expected jobs to be carried out to perfection. No screw-ups. No mistakes. No excuses.

She didn't suffer fools.

We always had a good professional relationship. I delivered my assignments on time and to the letter. Perhaps that was the only reason she indulged my call. Anyone else would have been instantly blacklisted.

"There were unforeseen complications," I said.

I wouldn't be able to stall for long, but I didn't feel comfortable coming right out and saying that I had no recollection of the last few days.

Isabella was my contact point at a black ops organization known as *Cobra Company*. It was an organization of former spooks and spec-war operators contracting jobs for government entities that wanted plausible deniability. There were plenty of on-the-books, legitimate contracts. Mostly private security details for high-profile government officials in foreign territories. But the organization also specialized in less public operations. High-value asset recovery. Snatch and grabs. Assassinations. Arming and training insurgent armies. All the types of things in which you would typically utilize spec-war operators. We were hired by the three-letter agencies on a regular basis. The benefit was no congressional oversight, and if things went wrong, no one got dirty.

But things often got complicated.

Sometimes you needed to prop up a local drug kingpin because his trafficking operation funded rebels who were going to topple the current dictator that you needed out of power.

War makes strange bedfellows.

"Your objective was to recover Julio Ruiz and bring him back to the United States for debrief. What part of that did you not understand?"

At least I knew what the objective was. Now I had to figure out what went wrong. The event was still an empty void in my memory.

"Are you hurt?"

"No," I lied.

"No? That's not what I hear?"

"What do you hear?"

"My sources say you were admitted to the hospital with a gunshot wound to the chest."

"Exaggeration. Merely a superficial wound from a low caliber weapon. No bone, no major arteries."

"Look, I'm going to shoot it to you straight because we have a long history," Isabella said. "You've always been a good performer. Cartwright said you lost control. He said you stormed into the room, shot the federal agents and the witness. He said he was forced to shoot you."

I was silent for a long moment, processing the information. "Cartwright is a terrible shot. And have you ever known me to lose control?"

After a moment, "No."

"Cartwright is lying."

"Why?"

"How should I know?"

Isabella was silent for a moment. "Where are you?"

"I'm not saying."

"As if I can't find out."

"I'll be gone by then."

"Come in for debrief."

"No."

Isabella sighed. "You're smarter than that, Tyson. Let me explain to you what happens if you don't come in."

"I know what happens if I don't come in."

"So, you're perfectly fine with being hunted by both the CIA and the cartels?"

"I'll take my chances. We both know that you have no choice but to take me out to save face. If you don't, the client will. Either way. It's bad for business if you let me live."

I put Isabella on speakerphone and changed into a white T-shirt, covered by a loud Hawaiian shirt, and cream cargo pants that hung in the closet. Every second counted, and I knew she was triangulating my position as we spoke. She knew what city I was in. It wouldn't be hard to pinpoint my exact location. Knowing Cobra Company, there were likely operatives close by. I expected a hit squad within the next few minutes.

"You're a valuable asset, Tyson. I hate to lose that."

"It's been fun, Isabella."

"Just one more thing..."

I cringed the moment she said it. I could tell by the tone in her voice she had something juicy to say.

"I know you're going to run. You're a good agent. You might even avoid capture for quite some time. But if you refuse to come in. I will be forced to use other means of persuasion."

"Elaborate."

"I believe your sister lives down in the Keys, doesn't she?"

I clenched my jaw. My blood boiled. "Leave her out of this."

"You know I have to exploit all available opportunities.

Make this easier on everyone. Come in, have a little chat, and nothing happens to your sister."

"I swear to God, if anything happens to her, you will regret it."

Isabella chuckled. "That's what I like about you, Tyson. You got balls."

She hung up the phone, and I knew they were coming.

I burst out of my hotel room with my pistol in the small of my back. Wearing dark sunglasses, a wide-brimmed hat, and a goofy outfit, I looked like every other tourist in the resort.

I took the battery out of the phone and tossed the device into the pool as I passed by.

The situation was all coming back to me, and it wasn't good. Ruiz was the head of one of the most powerful cartels in Mexico. The CIA had provided intel and assistance that allowed him to circumvent Customs, the FBI, and the Joint Interagency Task Force on drugs. They essentially gave him a free pass to ship billions of dollars worth of product into the United States. In exchange, the cartel supplied Venezuelan rebels with weapons and munitions. If that information ever became public knowledge, the political blowback would be catastrophic. Powerful people would do anything to keep it quiet.

It had long been speculated by various news outlets that the CIA was working with the Mexican and Colombian governments to intervene in Venezuela as it descended into a deepening crisis. They had spent considerable effort distributing funds to opposition groups and disseminating propaganda, as well as engaging in various PSYOPS. The US had a long history of meddling in Latin American affairs.

Speculation on interference was one thing. Proof of collusion with drug cartels was another.

I ambled up to the bar beside the pool. It was a thatched hut with every imaginable brand of flavored rum. I ordered a piña colada, sat on the barstool, and waited for the show to start. I was always a fan of hiding in plain sight.

Within a few minutes, four operatives descended on the resort—two from the north, two from the south, moving in a cover formation. They were locals who tried to look inconspicuous, but they stuck out like a sore thumb. They certainly weren't here for the surf and sand.

I watched as they made their way to the stairwell and ascended toward my room. I took a sip of the piña colada and pain stabbed through my chest. It hurt to do just about anything, but the stitches were holding, and other than some minor drainage, I wasn't bleeding much. The white T-shirt I had on under my Hawaiian shirt absorbed most of the blood before it spotted the loud print.

After a few moments, the hit squad emerged from my hotel room and made their way back across the property. One looked right at me on his way out.

It was like I was invisible.

Chalk one up for the tourist outfit.

There was no doubt that Isabella would have local operatives waiting at the airports, and my picture had probably been disseminated far and wide.

My cover identities were solid. I made them myself, so I knew Isabella didn't have them. I could book a commercial flight, but it would be risky. I needed to get back to the States as soon as possible and look after my sister. And I needed to prove to Isabella that I didn't fuck this operation up.

5

"Y ou are not going to believe the little honey I've got rolling now. She has got the sweetest little p—"

"Jack, I need you to focus," I said. "I have a little bit of a situation here."

I gave him the short version of the scenario.

Jack Donovan was an old Navy buddy of mine. He retired from the Teams as a Lieutenant Commander, then did a little private security consulting before getting out of the game entirely. Now he ran a charter boat service in the Keys. But he still had plenty of contacts at the CIA and DEVGRU.

He was the kind of guy that knew everybody, never met a stranger, and was full of tall tales—most of them had a grain of truth. He had long blonde hair that was well on its way to gray. He looked like an aging rock star and was confused for one on more than one occasion. He'd smile and sign autographs and accept the free drinks that came with it.

JD had a habit of dating women that were above the *no-go line* on the hot/crazy matrix. He seemed to like the drama.

The way I was dressed for my cover ID was the way Jack dressed on a daily basis—Hawaiian shirt over a T-shirt and cargo shorts. He had a leather jacket that was straight out of a '70s cop show that he wore to dress it up if he was going out at night.

He was the only person I knew I could trust. We had seen some pretty heavy combat together. Nothing like bullets to bond a friendship.

"Did I ever tell you about the time I went down to Cancún with Jeffery?"

"Focus, Jack!"

"Right, what do you need?"

"I need you to look after Madison."

"Madison's a firecracker. She doesn't need anybody looking after her."

"They're going to kill her if I don't cooperate," I said.

"In that case, I'll get right over there."

Madison owned *Diver Down*, a waterfront bar on Coconut Key Island.

"Also, I need a way back to the Keys as fast as possible."

JD thought about this for a moment. "You remember Tom Mahoney? Team guy. Tall. Sort of crooked nose."

I searched my mental archives. "Yeah. Operation Thunderstruck. Good guy."

"He retired to Playa. He's got a Cessna 172—flies tourists around on day trips. Let me give him a call and see what we can work out. He could probably have you back in the Keys in four hours. You'll have to go through Customs, but that won't be a problem, will it?"

"Not a problem. My cover ID is clean."

"From what you've told me, you're going to have every three-letter agency looking for you, as well as Cobra Company, and the cartel. Are you sure coming back here is such a good idea? I mean, we're just a hop skip and a jump from the Joint Interagency Task Force. There're all kinds of Feds running around down here."

"They threatened Madison."

"Isabella is a powerful enemy," JD cautioned.

"So am I."

There was a long pause.

"You should have gotten out of the business when you had the chance."

"Shoulda, coulda, woulda," I said.

JD made a few phone calls and set things up. I made my way up to Playa and connected with Tom Mahoney. His single-engine Cessna was painted like a World War II era bomber with aggressive shark-mouth nose art.

We met on the tarmac as he prepped his airplane. I winced when I shook his hand, and Mahoney instantly noticed my discomfort.

"Tom, good to see you. I really appreciate you doing this."

"Anything for a Team guy."

I hadn't seen him in nearly a decade and he had aged considerably. The sandy blonde haired man that I remembered had mostly gray hair now. His skin was tanned and leathery from too much sun. His blue eyes caught sight of a bloodstain seeping through my shirt. "Still in the business I take it?"

"Something like that."

"You don't look so good. Are you sure you're okay to fly?"

"It's nothing. Just a fishing accident."

Mahoney knew better. "I don't want to have to explain to the US customs why I've got a dead man in my passenger seat."

I tried to suppress a chuckle but failed. Another jolt of pain shot through my chest. "If I die on the trip just shove me into the ocean. No one's going to miss me. And it will frustrate the hell out of my enemies that they can't find me."

Mahoney laughed at that one. "Deal. I'm not gonna ask any more questions. The less I know the better." He paused for an uncomfortable moment. "I hate to bring it up, but... I did have to cancel my afternoon flights, and this trip is going to burn a lot of fuel. I understand if you're in trouble, but if you could—"

I stopped him right there. "Money is not an issue. How does $5,000 US sound?"

Depending on fuel prices, the cost to operate the plane was somewhere around $100 an hour when you factored in insurance, maintenance, and storage. The flight to Coconut Key was 457 nautical miles. With a top speed of 140 miles an hour, that would put us in Coconut Key in roughly 4 hours, give or take, depending on the weather and how hard Tom wanted to push it.

Mahoney's eyes brightened. "More than fair. That goes a long way down here." His initial enthusiasm quickly faded as he thought more about the offer. "Just how hot is your situation?"

"Hot enough."

"Let's get *wheels up* as soon as possible."

I agreed.

Mahoney went through his preflight checks and filed an ICAO flight plan. The weather was good and there were no storms in the Gulf. With any luck, it would be a smooth flight.

I hit the head before we left and bought a couple tacos for the trip. I also grabbed a pack of gum and bought a T-shirt that had two palm trees and a sunset and read: *Playa Del Carmen.* I wanted to have something to change into before we landed. A bloodstained shirt would arouse suspicion from the customs agents in Coconut Key.

It wasn't long before Mahoney had the single engine prop plane in the air over the Gulf. A wave of relief washed over me. I was relatively safe for the next several hours. Nobody was going to try to shoot at me up here.

6

The sun was dipping down over the horizon when we landed at the Coconut Key Municipal Airport. The amber globe sparkled the water and cast hues of pink and purple across the sky.

German shepherds sniffed around the airplane but didn't *indicate*. The Customs Agents looked over my passport. I was traveling as John McInerney. I flashed a brilliant smile, wearing my ridiculous Playa T-shirt. The customs agent looked me over and searched my travel bag. I had tossed out my pistol during the flight. No sense in raising eyebrows with a stolen weapon upon re-entry to the States. The only thing I had left in my zipper bag was a little bit of cash, two cell phones, and some chewing gum.

He waved me on, and that was that. Mahoney decided to refuel and fly right back. He had a full slate of tourist flights scheduled for the next day. I thanked him profusely, and he said to look him up the next time I was in Playa Del Carmen.

I didn't plan on going back anytime soon.

I called Jack and waited in the passenger pickup area. Within a few minutes, he pulled to the curb in a red Porsche 911 convertible—the wind blowing his long hair. Pop music pumped from the stereo. He yelled at me, "Get in, you vagrant."

It seemed like the charter business was treating JD well.

I pulled open the door and carefully slipped into the fine hand stitched leather of the bucket racing seats. The car was meticulously crafted. Black leather with red stitched seams, aluminum accents, racing steering wheel. I pulled the door closed, and it shut with a solid thunk. It didn't wobble or rattle. It was built like a tank.

JD dropped it into gear, and the flat-six cylinder launched us away from the terminal. He turned the stereo down to a level that was just slightly below the threshold for permanent shift hearing.

"Thanks, I owe you one," I shouted over the wind, music, and roar of the engine.

"Just trying to pay you back. I wouldn't be here if it weren't for you."

"Perhaps a slight exaggeration."

"Don't sell yourself short. That was a pretty hairy situation you pulled me out of back in Afghanistan."

"Ancient history, but I will graciously accept the return favor." I smiled. "How's Madison?"

"I went to happy hour at *Diver Down*. Everything's fine. No sign of trouble. I'll take you there now, but she's not going to be too happy to see you."

"I'll deal with that."

"Where are you planning on staying?"

I shrugged. "I figured I'd grab a room at the Beachcomber."

"Nonsense. You can crash on the couch at my place."

"Too dangerous. I've got some heavy hitters looking for me."

"I'm not afraid of a little danger."

"Yeah, but you got Scarlett to think about."

"You can crash on the *Slick'n Salty*."

I gave him a curious glance. There was no doubt about what the name was in reference to.

"45-footer. Master stateroom, guest stateroom, full bath, galley. All the comforts of home. I've got it docked in a slip at *Diver Down*. Power and water hookup. It's perfect for you. Plus, I could use a First Mate on some of these charters. That would be a way to earn your keep," he said with a sly wink. "I'll swing by my house and pick up the keys."

I appreciated the offer. But I wasn't sure how much time I would have to help JD out with fishing charters. But, it might be a good cover. I needed to lie low and watch over Madison, and that would put me in a prime spot.

"I made some calls to see what I could find out," JD said. "Nobody's saying much of anything."

"Cartwright set me up. He shot Ruiz and the Mexican Feds. It's all starting to come back to me now."

"Why? What's in it for him?"

"Maybe he got a better offer? I'll tell you one thing, when I get hold of him, he's going to wish he was dead."

It only took a few minutes to get to Jack's ocean-side house. The little 2-bedroom bungalow was right on the beach. The place could have been featured in Architectural Digest. It had a mid-century modern vibe, impeccably decorated. Floor-to-ceiling windows offered a stunning view of the crashing waves.

I took in the space, impressed. "You've done well for yourself, Jack."

He grinned. "Wait till you see the boat."

A stunning brunette sauntered out of a bedroom to see what the commotion was about. Her stiletto heels clacked against the hardwood floors, and her little black dress was painted on, leaving little to the imagination. The bottom of the dress rode high on her tanned, toned thighs. The girl was breathtaking.

Her bright eyes beamed at me. Before I knew it, she wrapped her arms around me and squeezed me tight.

I had no idea who it was.

"It's so good to see you, Tyson." She stepped back and looked me up and down. "Look at you, you're all grown up."

"Wait. Scarlett?"

She smiled. "In the flesh."

My eyes flicked to Jack.

He shrugged. "Who'd have thunk I could produce something like that?"

"You look so... different... from the last time I saw you," I stammered, still trying to process the transformation.

She snickered, knowing exactly what kind of effect she had on men. "Are you staying on the island long?"

"I'm not sure."

"Well, don't be a stranger." Her gorgeous eyes flicked to JD. "Jack, Chloe and I are going to *Sand Dunes.*"

"Be back at a reasonable hour. And stay out of trouble."

She grinned. "Always."

Scarlett had no intention of staying out of trouble.

She sauntered toward the door like a model prancing down the catwalk. A blonde in a convertible pulled in front of the house and Scarlett hopped into the car. The tires barked, and the two troublemakers sped away.

I looked at Jack like we were stuck in some weird episode of the Twilight Zone. "You let her out of the house like that?"

"You think I have any control over that monstrosity? She's got way too much of her mother in her."

7

"I don't understand. She was just a kid the last time I saw her?" I stood there, dumbstruck.

"You haven't been around in six years. Not since before..." JD quickly changed the subject not wanting to speak about the event. The thought he was trying to avoid had already flashed through my mind, and I knew I was going to have to deal with it sooner or later. But not now.

"And what's with this *Jack* thing. No more *Dad*?"

JD rolled his eyes. "Ever since the little miscreant turned 18, she's asserting her independence. She prefers to call me *Jack*. She also informed me that since she's an adult, we are now roommates. I said, okay, great, you can start paying for your half of the rent."

I chuckled, and my chest throbbed with pain.

"So far she hasn't taken me up on the offer. And this place ain't cheap."

"I can see that."

"You want a drink before we head over to *Diver Down?*"

"No thanks. I need to keep a clear head."

"Might take the edge off your pain. Besides, do you really want to confront Madison sober?"

"What do you have?"

"I've got everything," JD said with a wide smile. "You still drink that Bacardi 8 Year Reserve?"

"Tempting, but let's get to *Diver Down.*"

"Suit yourself."

"Oh, you got a gun I can borrow?"

Jack frowned at me. "The last thing I need to do is lend you one of my guns."

"I promise I won't kill anyone with it."

Jack scoffed. "I know better."

He slipped into the bedroom and returned a few moments later with an IWB Kydex holster that contained a Köenig-Haas MMX 9mm. He set the holster on the counter.

I picked it up, drew the weapon and press checked it. I dropped the magazine out and surveyed the rounds, then jammed the magazine back into the well. I made sure the weapon was on safe and slipped the pistol into the holster, then clipped it inside my waistband for an appendix carry. When I pulled my shirt over my waistband, it was nearly impossible to tell I was carrying.

"If you like that, you're going to love this," Jack said.

He disappeared into the bedroom and returned a few

moments later with a Köenig-Haas SA-25 semi-automatic, special applications sniper rifle.

It was a thing of beauty. Perfectly balanced, expertly crafted. I was no stranger to the weapon. They were popular with SOCOM units.

I admired the weapon for a moment, then handed it back to JD.

"And check this out," he said, holding three small surveillance cameras in the palm of his hand. They were no larger than shirt buttons. "These beauties are wireless. They'll connect to the Internet from anywhere. Initially, I thought I might put them up around the house when I went out of town to keep an eye on things. But you never know they might come in handy."

I looked at JD with a healthy dose of suspicion. "Don't tell me you're going to plant them in your ex-wife's house and spy on her."

"I would never dream of doing something like that," he said in an overly innocent tone.

This was coming from the guy who put a GPS tracker on his ex wife's car while they were still married. Granted, it *did* help him catch her cheating. My philosophy was if you had to go to such lengths to prove your spouse was cheating, you already knew what the outcome would be.

We hopped into Jack's midlife crisis and drove over to *Diver Down*. Madison and I inherited it after our folks' death, but I turned my share over to her. I didn't need the money, and I knew I was never going to be around to share the responsibility of running the place. I was off gallivanting around the globe, running covert ops.

Looking back, I'm not really sure what I was chasing. It seemed clear when I first joined the service. Like many, I wanted to serve my country and challenge myself. See what I was made of. Be a part of something bigger than myself. Of course, there was the added bonus of shooting guns, jumping out of planes, and blowing things up.

After six years as an Officer in the Teams, I wanted to be more directly involved with the intelligence community. I wanted to serve as more than just a tactical unit. I applied for a position as a Paramilitary Operations Officer with the CIA. A lot of people tried to talk me out of it. Said I'd be happier where I was, and that it was doubtful I'd passed the poly and the background check, anyway.

I knew I was pretty clean. I hadn't done drugs in the last five years. I had no relationships with any operatives of foreign governments. There wasn't anything egregious in my past that anyone could use to blackmail me. I admitted to all the minor indiscretions that I made as a youth. The time I got a *Minor in Possession of Alcohol* at a high school football game. Selling old term papers to underclassmen. And the time I used gasoline to draw a giant penis in the grass on our rival's football field before the big game.

That made the cute blonde administering the poly blush.

Miraculously, I passed the poly, and the background check, and received a 5-year contract. By the end of the term, I had been approached by Cobra Company to do essentially the same thing, but for way more money. At the time, it was a no-brainer. But that's when things started to get complicated.

Now, at 35, I felt lost.

Cobra Company wasn't just a private clandestine contractor. They had grown into a powerful, connected organization that was well-funded. And they had a degree of immunity. It was in everyone's best interest to let the company operate without much scrutiny. Many governmental agencies preferred not to notice when Cobra Company did something of questionable legality. And the company drifted into more and more gray areas of operation. Cobra Company became a vault that held a lot of nasty secrets that no one wanted exposed.

And I could expose a lot of them.

The muffled sound of music spilled into the parking lot as we pulled up to *Diver Down*. The neon sign on the front facade buzzed, and the fresh sea breeze blew my hair. It was your typical beach town restaurant and bar. Lots of deck work, life preservers on the wall for decoration, palm trees, thatched roofs. A stunning view of the ocean on one side, and the marina on the other. It was the best spot on the island for a bar. It drew a mix of tourists and regulars.

I strolled inside, took a seat at the bar, and waited for the fireworks to begin.

8

M adison's seething eyes blazed into me. There were a lot of things she was pissed off at me about. "See that sign. It says that I have the right to refuse service to anyone. So why don't you pick yourself up, turn around, and walk out of here. We'll both be better off."

Madison had golden blonde hair that was highlighted by the sun. She had olive skin, sculpted cheekbones, and blue eyes that had broken many hearts. She had been a model and a professional surfer until she blew out her knee. After two ACL reconstructions, she decided it was best to retire from the board if she wanted to continue to walk without a limp.

It seemed like she hadn't aged a day since the last time I saw her. She wore a bikini top and jean shorts and didn't have any intention of wearing anything else. She wasn't a 9-to-5'er, and loathed putting on shoes, much less business attire. The bar was her life. She was 31 now, and she had taken over the bar just about the time she aged out of modeling. *It's a cruel business where you're washed up at 25.*

"I was just in the neighborhood. Thought I'd say hello." I wasn't about to tell her about my situation, or that she was in danger. It would only enrage her further.

A big burly guy marched toward me. He had curly brown hair and a beard. Barrel chested guy, wearing a T-shirt, cargo shorts, and flip-flops. He practically snarled at me. "This guy giving you trouble, Maddy?"

"He was just leaving," she said.

"You heard the lady. Get your ass up and get out of here."

A thin, almost imperceptible, smile tugged at my lips. I was amused, partially by the fact this guy had no idea who he was dealing with. But I was also appreciative that he was looking out for Madison.

"Look, buddy, there's no problem here. I'm her brother."

"I don't give a shit who you are. Family reunion is over."

I chuckled.

"Is there something funny about that?" the Burly Guy asked.

"It's okay Jeremy. I can handle this," Maddy said.

Jeremy seemed disappointed. "Are you sure? Because I'd love to smash his face in."

He tried to appear menacing with crazed eyes. He kept staring at me and didn't break eye contact.

"Let me buy you a beer, Jeremy," I said.

"I'll take a long neck so I can shove it up your ass," he growled.

"Sounds kinky, but I'm not really into that kind of thing."

That pissed him off.

He cocked his fist back ready to swing. Normally, it would have been a big mistake on his part, but I was in no condition to fight. Fortunately, Madison stopped him. "Jeremy! I got this."

Jeremy exhaled and reluctantly backed away. "You holler if you need anything, Maddy. I got your back."

"I know you do," Madison said with a wink.

Her vicious gaze turned back to me. "What are you doing here?"

"I guess now's not a good time to mention I'll be living on Jack's boat."

Her eyes widened. "Oh, no you're not. You can find another slip if that's the case."

"It's just temporary."

"I wouldn't expect you to actually put down roots anywhere," she said, her voice dripping with sarcasm.

"Who knows? Maybe I'll stay awhile this time?"

"No, you won't."

She was silent for a moment as the rage built. "You didn't even come back for their funeral, Tyson. You left me here to deal with everything on my own. You have no idea how hard that was."

"I was on assignment. I couldn't come back. You know that."

Her eyes brimmed. "And after the assignment? You just washed your hands of everything."

"The last time I talked to you on the phone you said don't bother coming home. *If I never see you again, it will be too soon*, you said. I wanted to honor your wishes."

Madison slumped, her word spit back to her. She took in a deep breath and steeled her resolve. "See, you can't even keep a simple promise."

I grimaced. "Come on, JD. I think we can find another slip over at Pirates' Cove."

I pushed away from the bar and marched out of the establishment.

Jack shrugged to Madison. "You guys need to work that shit out. Life is short."

I tried to decompress in the parking lot. Jack caught up with me. "I'll call Bobby and see if he's got room in the cove for a 45-footer." He dialed his cell phone. As he waited for an answer, he said, "Damn, son. That woman can hold a grudge."

"Well, that's not the only thing she's pissed off at me about."

A voice crackled through the speaker on JD's phone. Bobby had space available, and within a few moments Jack had negotiated a deal. "Sounds great. We'll see you in about an hour."

"Man, I didn't mean to put you through all this trouble. Let's just forget about it. I'll grab a room. Just keep the boat here."

"Ain't no big deal," JD said. "But Bobby does want $100 more a month."

I felt even worse. "I'll cover it."

"Damn right you will."

"Not like you need me to. Looks like you've got deep pockets."

Jack smiled. "Life is good."

9

"**A**in't she a beauty?" Jack said, beaming with pride as he showed me the *Slick'n Salty*.

It was a hell of a fishing boat. No doubt about it. It must have cost a fortune—at least half a million on the used market.

Water lapped against the fiberglass hull of the boat. Mooring lines creaked and groaned.

We climbed over the transom into the cockpit. There was a bait prep center and sink with both freshwater and a raw water wash down system. The deck house alone was luxuriously appointed with cherry cabinetry and indirect lighting. There was a large flat panel display and a surround sound stereo with subwoofer. There was an L-shaped lounge with padded cushions, and an L-shaped dinette. The galley was fitted with a microwave, cooktop, sink, fridge, quartz countertops, and cherry cabinetry. The bridge deck was above the deck house and had its own stereo system, bench seats, and storage. Two 16,000 BTU air conditioning units could handle just about anything the Florida summer could throw at it.

"The twin cat C-18 diesel engines are putting out about 2030 hp total. She'll run, and run good."

I was in awe. "How did you afford this?"

"I saved my pennies. Plus, this thing has been a gold mine." He leaned in and whispered, "I gotta be honest. I'm not just doing fishing charters."

My mind instantly went to somewhere it shouldn't. But JD wasn't the type to do anything *too* illegal. At least, I didn't think he was.

"I'm catering to the rich and psuedo-famous."

My face twisted, perplexed. "What do you mean?"

"These goddamn millennials got more money than sense. These social media *influencers* come down here, charter the boat. I take them out on the water and let them party, fish, whatever. They'll pay just about whatever I charge. They take their pictures and hashtag it all over the Internet, and all that does is bring me more business. Plus, these honeys soak up the sun on the deck, and most of the time the bikinis come right off. God forbid they have a tan line. I feel like I've died and gone to heaven."

I chuckled. This lifestyle was right up JD's alley. Hell, it was right up anybody's alley.

JD unhooked the power and water and we were close to casting off when Madison sauntered down the dock. "Alright. You can stay. On one condition."

She caught me off guard. I didn't expect her to back down. "Name it."

"We've had a few break-ins around here. Nothing major. A few stereo systems boosted. Fishing rods. That kind of thing. If you're living on the boat, just keep an eye out for people who don't belong."

"Easy enough."

"And one more thing."

"Anything."

She thought about it for a moment. "We'll talk more about it later."

Madison spun around and marched back down the dock.

I wondered what I had gotten myself into.

"I'll call Bobby and let him know there's been a change of plans," JD said.

We spent the rest of the evening sitting in the salon, watching the game, drinking rum. It was doing a moderate job of numbing the pain in my chest. By this time, the left side of my neck was black and blue and was visible above my T-shirt. The swelling was so bad it was compressing the nerves at the brachial plexus and I was getting tingling sensations in my fingertips. I alternated an ice pack 10 minutes on and 10 minutes off.

"Do you think you can score some antibiotics?"

"I can score anything. Need some Vicodin? I've got some around here from my knee surgery."

He fumbled around and came up with a half-empty bottle

of pills and tossed them to me. Hydrocodone. *Do not consume alcohol or operate heavy machinery.* I popped two and washed them down with a rum and cola.

My cell phone buzzed in my pocket. The only person that had this number was JD.

Unknown caller.

I cringed, but decided I better answer the call. I knew who it was. There was only one person it could be, unless it was a wrong number.

"So good to hear from you, Isabella. I thought we had said our goodbyes?"

"Well, no matter how hard I try to stay away, I'm always drawn back to you."

"I'm flattered. How did you get this number?"

"I have my ways. Did you enjoy your flight?"

"I don't know what you're talking about."

"Cut the crap. The only reason you're not dead right now is because I'm keeping them at bay."

"The only reason I'm not dead right now is because I'm smarter than you."

"Are you trying to get on my bad side?"

"I thought I already was. I saw the little hit squad you sent for me. Amateurs."

"Yes, well, I've had a change of heart."

"Shocking. I didn't know you had a heart."

She ignored my gibe. "Cartwright has gone radio silent."

"What does that tell you?" I said with an air of superiority.

"It tells me that maybe we both got played."

"So you believe me when I say that I didn't kill Ruiz."

"You know I'm not that trusting. But I'm calling off the dogs right now until I can get something more concrete."

"That's mighty kind of you."

"I want you to stay in Coconut Key until I get this sorted. I've got agents tracking Cartwright now."

I grimaced at the fact that she knew where I was. "Cartwright's good. You might not find him. But if you do, I want a piece of him."

"I found you, didn't I? Our client is willing to back off until more information comes to light."

"Follow the money. It will lead to the truth. I know you have ways of finding untraceable bank accounts. Find Cartwright's and look for any large deposits."

"I don't need you to tell me how to do my job. And if he turned on me, I hope he did it for a lot of money. And speaking of bank accounts... Your assets have been frozen. Sorry. Not my doing."

My fist tightened, and I clenched my jaw. "Anything else?"

"Stay off the radar. No freelance work. No trouble. Stay in plain sight. Our client will get nervous if you become unavailable." Isabella paused for a moment. "I can't do anything about the cartels. So watch your back. Ruiz's people will be coming for you."

The line went dead.

I breathed a small sigh of relief. At least Cobra Company wasn't coming for me, or Madison, yet. And I didn't have to worry about the Feds for the moment.

I knew the drill. I was an asset that could become a liability. An operative gone rogue can create havoc for those who wish to keep secrets. My fate would depend upon what Isabella's investigation turned up.

As much as I wanted to track down and kill Cartwright, it was best if Isabella found him and *debriefed* him. I needed her to come to the conclusion on her own that I didn't kill Ruiz. Then she would have to sell that fact to our client.

JD was curious, so I filled him in on the details of the conversation. For the next few weeks, I didn't hear anything more from Isabella. No cartel hitmen showed up. Everything seemed reasonably calm. My wound had scabbed over and didn't get infected.

I had learned the world's worst thing for an injury was to let the surrounding muscles atrophy. I started with isometrics. After 10 days, I removed the stitches myself and began doing very light range of motion activities, gradually moving up to 2-pound weights. The movement kept the scar tissue from getting too nasty and increased blood flow, which meant faster healing. I did a lot of soft tissue massage, trying to break up the chunky scar, and I kept bumping up weights as tolerated.

As an operator, you learned to rehab injuries and keep your body conditioned. I was lucky the injury was mostly superficial.

It was the off-season, so JD didn't have many charters. I wasn't in any condition to assist, so most of the time I'd stay behind at *Diver Down* and try not to annoy my sister. I'd watch the boats of the marina come and go. I'd take walks on the beach, eat cheeseburgers, and drink piña coladas. It was like a strange vacation—the first time in my life I had experienced any real extended leisure time.

Once the stitches were out, I was usually up by 5 AM and out for a morning run, and apart from my rehab exercises, the rest of the day was generally lazy. In the evenings, JD would swing by and we'd share a beer or a cocktail, and quite often he persuaded me to venture out for some local nightlife.

JD may have been close to 50, maybe a little bit over. He had an uncanny ability to approach total strangers and become their best friend within minutes. He was the kind of guy that wherever he went he was the life of the party. Men liked him and women were intrigued by his charm. He was always buying rounds of shots, which may have added to his likability factor. But he had no shortage of women half his age wanting personal attention from him.

It didn't take long for me to decide that I was done with the spy trade. I had been moving so fast for my entire life that I never really stopped and took a chance to live. All of my relationships had suffered. I wasn't really sure what I was going to do with the rest of my life. Maybe I could stay here in the Keys forever?

The farther I got away from my near-death experience, the more I tried to write it off as a hallucination. The paranoid dreams of a traumatized mind. But I knew deep down inside it was as real as anything I had ever experienced. And I probably wouldn't find much redemption being a lazy beach bum on Coconut Key Island.

But sometimes life is funny about giving you exactly what you need—*whether you realize it or not.* I may have been done with adventure, but adventure wasn't done with me.

10

A bloodcurdling scream echoed across the water. It sounded like Madison. The shrill tone filtered in through the open hatch, startling me. My heart leapt into my throat. I had been sitting in the salon watching a Netflix documentary on a man who was railroaded by the cops and convicted of a murder he didn't commit.

I sprang from my seat, dashed across the cockpit, hopped over the transom, and sprinted down the dock. By the time I reached the parking lot, a crowd had gathered around.

It wasn't Madison who screamed. It was another young woman. She told me at first she thought a bird had shit on her. Then she realized it was something much worse. She stared with horrified eyes at a bloody eyeball that lay on the asphalt. It had dropped from the sky, bounced off her shoulder, then smacked the ground.

I glanced around and saw several birds swooping into the alley behind the bar by the dumpsters. When I rounded the corner, I saw a bird pecking at the body of a big burly man. As I drew closer, I recognized Jeremy.

The scavengers fluttered away, launching into the sky as I approached. Flies buzzed around the corpse. His skin had a greenish tinge to it, and his shirt was stained with blood. From what I could tell without a close examination, he had multiple stab wounds to the chest and neck.

I kept the crowd back, trying to preserve the crime scene until Sheriff Daniels arrived. Before long, camera flashes from the forensics team illuminated the alley as they chronicled and catalogued the scene. The medical examiner, Brenda Sparks, put the time of death within the last two hours. Sheriff Daniels interviewed the bar patrons as well as Madison and me. Since I discovered the body, I was the witness he spent the most time with.

Madison was pretty shaken up. She had burst into tears upon the sight of Jeremy's body. She wasn't used to seeing this kind of carnage.

"Was there anything going on between you two?" Sheriff Daniels asked Madison.

Her face twisted. "No. I mean, he asked me out a few times. I said no."

"Why did you say no?"

"I don't date customers."

"How did he take the rejection?"

Madison shrugged.

"What does this have to do with anything?" I asked.

"Just trying to get a sense of your relationship. He was killed on your property after all."

"He seemed disappointed, but not overly so," Madison said. "He continued to be a customer. He was in just about every day."

"And where were you when this happened?" the sheriff asked.

Madison's brow crinkled. "You don't think I had something to do with this, do you?"

"These are just routine questions."

"Madison's not going to answer any more questions without a lawyer," I said.

"I don't need a lawyer," she protested. "I didn't do anything. Jeremy was a friend. I want to do anything I can to help find the person who did this."

"I thought you said he was just a customer," Sheriff Daniels said, almost accusingly.

"I didn't think there was a law against being friends with your customers," Madison said.

"Just so I can rule you out, where were you at the time of death?"

"Since I don't know when the time of death was, I don't think I can accurately answer that. But I've been inside that bar behind the counter trying to make sure my customers get served their food on time, and that their glasses are never empty. I've got an entire waitstaff that can verify my whereabouts."

"Was there any time that you left the bar? Maybe to take the trash out?"

"No. I don't take the trash out when I'm serving food. One of the busboys usually does that."

"Who's bussing today?"

"Pete Mitchell."

Sheriff Daniels wrote the information down in a small pocket notebook. His suspicious eyes flicked to me. This blowhard was getting on my nerves. I had run into many local cops like this before. Guys who liked to throw their weight around every opportunity they could. "What about you? What's your story?"

I knew better than to talk to the police. They could take anything you said and twist it out of context. Opening your mouth to law enforcement is just giving the prosecution ammunition. Most criminals would get away with their crimes if they would just shut the hell up. But criminals have a bad habit of thinking they're smarter than everyone else. Newsflash, no one ever talked their way out of a crime, but they sure as hell talked their way into a conviction.

The last thing I needed in my current situation was the local sheriff on my ass. Even though I had grown up in Coconut Key, I was new to town. In Sheriff Daniels's eyes, I was an outsider.

I wanted to appear cooperative. "I was on the boat when I heard a scream. I ran to the parking lot. Then I found the body in the alleyway. That's all I know. And if you have any questions beyond that, I'd be happy to answer them in the presence of my attorney."

"Only the guilty lawyer up," the sheriff said with attitude.

I tried not to show my disdain for the man. Sheriff Daniels was the type of guy who would do anything to make himself look good. I wouldn't put it past him to manufacture evidence, or ignore exculpatory facts.

"Which boat?" Daniels asked.

"The *Slick'n Salty*. I pointed toward the marina."

"Jack Donovan's boat?" he asked as he looked past my shoulder at the row of boats."

I nodded.

"That's a long way. I imagine it would be hard to hear a scream at that distance."

"Voices carry over the water."

"What exactly is it that brings you back to town?"

"The friendly locals," I said, my voice thick with sarcasm.

11

I finally decided to take my own advice and shut the hell up. I had already said too much as it was. I understand why people talk. When a smug asshole gets in your face, you want to tell him his suspicions are wrong. Being accused of something you didn't do is maddening. But cops see the world with different eyes. It comes with the job. There are two kinds of people in the world. Those who are *on the job*, and everybody else. And everybody else is a potential suspect.

Work in law enforcement for long enough and you will come to the conclusion that anyone is capable of anything, given the right circumstances. You tend to see the worst aspects of humanity. It's like being a spy. Work in the trade for too long, and you'll never trust anyone again.

When the sheriff figured he wasn't going to get much more out of me, he moved on to interview other witnesses. He decided not to bring me down to the station for further questioning. He probably didn't want the extra paperwork.

He didn't have enough grounds to arrest me, and truth be told, I don't think he wanted to work that hard, anyway. He sure as hell hadn't made any headway on my parents' murders in the six years that the case had been sitting on his desk.

Madison and I were primary beneficiaries of my parents' estate. That also made us suspects, even though it was clear we had nothing to do with their deaths. On more than one occasion, I had voiced my displeasure with Daniels's line of questioning and his lack of action in regard to the case. It hadn't put us on the best terms.

Madison closed *Diver Down* for the rest of the evening. She needed a little time to decompress. I called JD, and he came over as soon as he could. The three of us sat on the deck in *Diver Down*, drinking beer.

"I still can't believe he's dead," Madison said, staring at her beer bottle, peeling the soggy label from the amber bottle as it sweat. "Who would do such a thing? Here of all places?"

"This island ain't exactly what it used to be," JD said.

"But we've never had a problem here," Madison replied.

"Did Jeremy have any enemies?" I asked.

"Not that I know of. I mean, I didn't know him that well. But he was in here just about every day."

"His watch was stolen," I said.

"How do you figure that?" Madison asked.

"Tan line on the wrist."

"Maybe it was a robbery gone wrong?" JD said.

"Maybe," I said. "Whoever did this didn't want Jeremy talking to anyone about it afterward. That's for certain. As soon as the carotid artery was severed, he was gone."

"He was a big boy, too," JD added.

"Not an obvious target for a mugging," I said. "There are much easier targets around here."

I asked Madison where Jeremy worked.

She said, "He sometimes works for Dan Baker aboard the *Homewrecker*. But it doesn't seem steady."

"Does he have a girlfriend?" I asked.

"I don't think so. I mean, he asked me out."

"Doesn't mean anything," I replied.

Madison's eyes narrowed at me. "That's cynical."

"That's life."

"You can't go through life thinking everybody's going to fuck you over," Madison said.

"It's worked out well so far."

"Really?" Madison asked, incredulous.

"I'm still alive."

"But you've hurt a lot of people around you with that attitude."

"What are you talking about?"

She huffed. "Total narcissist. Completely unaware how your actions affect other people."

"Did I miss something here?" I asked.

"Does anyone need another beer?" JD asked, wanting to avoid the drama.

"Yeah," I said.

JD scurried away.

"You want to tell me what you're getting at?" I asked.

"Hannah really liked you," Madison said.

I sighed. "You're still mad about that?"

"Yes. She was my best friend."

"I didn't want her to get hurt. So, I—"

"Pushed her away."

I grimaced. I couldn't argue. "Maybe," I sighed with resignation.

I was notorious for pushing people away who got too close. My lifestyle wasn't conducive to settling down. And having ties made me vulnerable, not to mention it was dangerous for anyone who cared about me.

"Next time, maybe you should let other people decide how much of you they can take."

JD returned with a few more beers. "Is it safe?"

Madison shot him a look.

I wanted to change the subject as quickly as possible. "Maybe we should pay this Dan Baker a visit?"

"Don't you have enough trouble as it is without poking around this?" JD asked.

"This kind of thing is bad for business," I said.

"Sheriff Daniels is useless," Madison said. "In six years he hasn't made any headway on the case, and the people who killed Mom and Dad are still out there. This will get filed away just like every other major crime on this island. Oh sure, he'll stomp around, ask questions, and pretend like he's working. But that will last a week. Then Jeremy will be forgotten."

"I'll look into this. I can't make any promises, but if they're on this island, I'll find your friend's killer."

For the first time since I'd been on the island, Madison gave me a look of appreciation.

She was silent for a long moment. "Since we're on the subject of murder, what do you know about Mom and Dad?"

Her eyes were already starting to brim.

"I know what you know."

"Surely, with all your contacts and resources, you know something?"

"I looked into it. I followed every lead. I had friends in the bureau look into it. I got nothing. The way I see it, one of two things happened. They were shot and killed for their boat. Or they stumbled across drug smugglers. Or both."

Madison looked tortured.

"The boat was never found," I said.

"You think it's pointless to keep looking," she said, accusingly.

"No. But there comes a time where you have to accept facts. We might not ever find out what happened to them, or who did it."

"Promise me you won't stop trying," she pleaded.

12

J D and I caught Dan Baker the next morning at the Pirate's Cove Marina before he set out on his charter. I figured it would be good to have Jack with me since Dan knew him. He was prepping the boat and filling dive tanks. He invited us both aboard without hesitation. We hopped the transom and stepped into the cockpit. He had a nice Valkyrie 63-footer.

"What can I do for you boys?" Dan asked.

Dan was mid 50s, wavy brownish gray hair, mustache, and a full beer belly. He hobbled from a bad hip, but it didn't seem to slow him down.

"We'd like to talk to you about Jeremy Phelps," I said, getting straight to the point.

Dan looked at his watch. "Well, if he doesn't get here in the next five minutes, he's going to be looking for another job."

"You haven't heard?" I asked.

"Heard what?"

"You mean Sheriff Daniels hasn't spoken with you?" JD asked.

"No. What's this about?"

I told him that Jeremy had been killed, but I left out pertinent details.

Dan hung his head. "That's a damn shame. Jeremy was a good kid. A little bit of a slacker, but his heart was in the right place. Never on time though."

"How long had he been working for you?" I asked.

"I guess going on three years now. Mostly part-time. He wasn't reliable enough to bring on full-time." He paused for a moment, then surveyed me a little closer. "Are you some type of private investigator?"

"He was a friend of my sister's," I said.

"I don't need a lawyer or anything, do I?" He was half joking.

"Just asking a few questions. Can you think of anyone who might have wanted to do Jeremy harm? Did he have a beef with anyone?"

Dan thought about it for a moment. "Not that I'm aware of. But, to be honest, I really only saw him when he showed up to work on the boat. I couldn't tell you much about his personal life. I think he still dates Catherine. *Dated*," he corrected himself. "Can't think of her last name. She's a waitress at *Craig's Crab and Claw*."

"Do you know if they were having any issues?" I asked.

"I don't get involved in the personal drama of my employees. And I don't let them bring it on the boat."

There were a couple of fillet knives in the bait prep area. Nice ones. Titanium nitride coated blades. I didn't have a chance to really examine Jeremy's body, but they looked like they could be consistent with the wounds on Jeremy's torso and neck. But so could a million other fillet knives in the area.

"Where were you yesterday?" I asked.

"Now I'm really starting to feel like I need a lawyer."

"Nobody's accusing you of anything, Dan," JD said, realizing he needed to diffuse the situation. "It's just a standard question to cross you off the list."

Dan frowned. He didn't like answering the question, but he decided it was probably in his best interest. "I was out on the water most of the day, running a fishing charter. If you need to corroborate that, talk to my first mate." Dan called up to the bridge. "Luke, where was I yesterday?"

A guy in his mid-20s leaned over the rail. He had brown hair, tan skin, and abs that belonged on an underwear model. "Uh, you were on the boat, Captain."

"What time did we get back to the marina?"

"I don't know, maybe 6:30? Then it took at least an hour for cleanup."

"Satisfied?" Dan said, glaring at me.

I didn't say anything.

"After that, I took some ibuprofen, popped a muscle relaxer, and had a few beers. I got a hip that needs to be replaced and I'm just waiting on the insurance to approve it. Do I look like I'm in any condition to assault a young man of Jeremy's size?"

"Nobody said you did," I said.

"Well, you sure are poking around like you've already made up your mind."

"I apologize if it came across that way. I'm just trying to get to the bottom of this," I said.

"If there's anybody I've got a reason to kill, it's my ex-wife," Dan said. "And she's still breathing. Unfortunately. She took just about everything I own, and all I got left is this boat. And I'm upside down on that."

"I feel your pain, brother," JD said.

"Maybe you ought to leave the investigating to the Sheriff?" Dan said.

"I don't see him out here," JD said.

"Better look again," Dan said, pointing to the parking lot.

Sheriff Daniels's cruiser just pulled up.

I thanked Dan for his time and we left. We crossed paths with the sheriff halfway down the dock. His narrow eyes glared at us. "What are you boys doing out here?"

"I'm looking for another slip for the boat," JD said. "Thought I'd ask Dan how he likes things out here."

The sheriff knew better. "Let me give you boys a little piece of advice. Mind your own business. You wouldn't want to be obstructing a criminal investigation, would you? I got this thing handled."

I had to bite my tongue. He sure hadn't handled my parents' investigation worth a damn.

We continued on our way, albeit a little more briskly. There was no doubt Dan would probably bitch about us to the sheriff.

"Do you think you could work your charm with Brenda Sparks?" I asked. "Maybe get a copy of the ME's report?"

A wry smile tugged on Jack's lips. "You know I can get just about anything I need out of anybody. But Sheriff Daniels is not going to be happy if he finds out."

"Then make sure he doesn't find out?"

13

J D was right. He had a sweet gig. I thought he had been exaggerating, but the scenery was more than I could have imagined.

We had a charter client that afternoon, and I finally felt well enough to assist. I figured it was time I started earning my keep. I hadn't paid Jack anything for rent, and I had been sponging off Madison. She had been generous enough to extend me a tab at *Diver Down* until I could get access to my cash.

A good operative keeps multiple caches of weapons, supplies, and cash in case of emergency. I had one in the area, but I hadn't been able to get to it. I was planning to make a visit to my stash, now that I was capable.

Four insanely hot girls boarded the boat wearing string bikinis that barely covered anything. Tight fabric struggled to contain perky assets. Their tanned, oiled skin glistened in the tropical sunlight. The smell of coconut wafted from their perfect bodies, flat stomachs, and toned legs. Each one had model good looks.

"Told you," Jack said, nudging an elbow into my ribs.

There was a blonde, a brunette, a redhead, and a sandy blonde with a pixie cut. They all wore sunglasses and had wide-brimmed hats. They had already started on the fruity drinks—strawberry daiquiris were the flavor of the moment.

They wanted to party, soak up the sun, and bar hop across the island.

I unhooked the lines, and we cast off. We weren't even out of the bay before bikini tops came off.

This was going to be an exercise in mental focus. I tried not to let my eyes wander, but a topless woman has a certain magnetic quality about her.

The day started out pretty smooth, but that changed after the first stop. After a short cruise, we pulled to the dock at *Riptide*. It was a popular tourist spot where you could get buckets of ice cold beer and fresh seafood. Crab, lobster, and crawfish, when in season. Music pumped, and the smell of spilled beer filled the air.

The girls disembarked and mingled about the bar. We were just the hired help, so we stayed onboard and waited until it was time to shuttle them to the next destination. Neither of us drank while operating the boat. That would be bad business and asking for trouble. We saved our cocktails for after we were back in the marina.

By the time the girls returned they had indulged in a few too many daiquiris and tequila shots. Hot girls don't leave clubs alone, and they had four guys in tow. Typical muscle heads wearing board shorts and gold chains, all with the same haircut.

Jack and I exchanged a glance and rolled our eyes. Few things are more annoying than being the sober person around a bunch of drunk idiots—it doesn't matter how hot they are.

They were loud, bratty, and their music was terrible. Maybe I was just getting old. While we were still docked at *Riptide*, one of the guys dropped his shorts and pissed over the back of the transom. I told him to use the head next time. That didn't go over well.

"Excuse me," the brunette snapped. "We paid good money for this boat. If he wants to drop his pants, he can drop his pants." She had a lascivious glint in her eyes.

I didn't want to start shit on JD's boat. I decided to disengage and walk away. But then she had to push things.

"Hey, you. Get me a beer!" No *please*. No *thank you*. Her voice was thick with condescension.

"Excuse me?"

"You heard her," the douche-canoe said. "Get her a beer."

I forced a smile. "I'm sorry. I'm not a servant."

"Like I said. I'm paying good money for premium service. If I want you to get me a beer, you'll get me a beer."

"Get it yourself," I said.

The douche-canoe puffed up his chest like he was going to do something.

JD saw the incident and rushed to me before things got out of hand. "Hey now, what's the trouble here?"

"Your deckhand refuses to serve me," the brunette snapped.

"One beer coming right up," JD said with a smile. "Can I get anybody else anything?"

Jack didn't have a liquor license. Drinks were free on the boat. He more than made up for it with the price of the charter.

JD took my arm and pulled me into the deck house. "If you haven't figured it out, this is a service industry. We do what the client wants. Besides, that girl has 2 million followers."

"What do I give a shit how many followers she has?"

"Pull your head out of your ass. That girl is a major source of revenue. I'll have a dozen more of her supermodel friends down here next week once they see her pictures all over the Internet."

I exhaled. "Fine. I'll play nice. The service industry was never my bag."

I grabbed a beer from the fridge and delivered it to the bratty brunette. She snapped a picture of me as I handed the bottle to her.

"What are you doing?" I asked.

"Posting to my followers how horrible the service is on this boat."

I'm usually calm, cool, and collected under pressure. But I couldn't have my picture floating around the Internet. I snatched the brat's phone and tossed it into the ocean. It plunked into the water and sunk to the bottom of the channel.

That drew quite the reaction.

"What the actual fuck?" she exclaimed. "That was my phone!"

It was like I had taken away the most important thing in the world.

That's when the douche-canoe made a big mistake. His palms smacked against my chest as he shoved me across the cockpit. It caught me off balance, and I stumbled back.

I managed to regain my footing. The wound in my chest had mostly healed, but there was a twinge of discomfort from the contact. My instincts took over, and I was ready to neutralize the threat, but fortunately JD stepped in. "Hey now, this isn't a contact sport."

"He threw my phone in the water!" the brat complained. "This is the worst party boat I've ever been on. That phone cost $1,000."

"I'm terribly sorry," JD apologized, flashing a disarming smile. "My deckhand is new, and a little socially awkward."

I glared at him, but kept my mouth shut.

"Today's charter is on me," JD said. "And I'll reimburse you for the phone. How does that sound?"

She thought about it for a moment. "Well, I guess it's okay." She pointed to me. "But I want him off the boat."

14

"Tyson, you're fired!" Jack said.

The bratty brunette smiled.

JD made a big show of it. "Now get up to the bridge deck and stay there."

I gave him a mock salute, "Aye-aye, Captain."

JD turned back to the brat. "I'm really sorry about his behavior. He's never working this boat again. But I need to keep him on board for the duration of the charter, just in case we need an extra hand. But I promise, he'll stay out of your way."

That seemed to appease her for the time being.

We idled away from *Riptide*, and JD brought the *Slick'n Salty* on plane once we got into open water.

The tourism board billed the Keys as a boater's paradise. But they could quickly become a boater's nightmare. There were over 6,000 reefs and 800 keys in the area. Depths changed rapidly. One minute the draft would be seven feet, the next three. *Say hello to new propellers.* The key to staying out of trouble was to study the charts, use your GPS, follow the markers, and stay out of areas you didn't know well. Venture into the wrong area and rake across a bed of protected seagrass, and you might end up owing a hefty fine for destroying a sanctuary.

We headed south toward *Action Stations*. It had good food and a great view of the sunset. The winds picked up, and it was starting to get a little choppy.

JD had instructed everyone to stay in either the cockpit or the salon while we were underway. It used to be illegal to ride on the bow while moving at anything above an idle, but Florida HB 703 changed that. Now it wasn't considered *Careless Operation* if passengers rode on the bow. An aluminum bow rail enclosed the area, but it still wasn't a good idea.

The bratty brunette decided she wanted to play *Titanic* and feel the wind blowing through her hair from the bow. But the minute she climbed onto the gunwale, her foot slipped and she splashed into the water. She was lucky she didn't crack her head on the gunwale, or get chopped up in the propellers.

I watched the event happen in slow motion. I tapped JD on the shoulder and told him to slow the boat down and spin around.

The brat splashed and flailed in the water.

She couldn't swim.

I dove from the bridge into the water and swam toward her. The other ass-clowns just stood around gawking. By the time I reached the girl, she had slipped underwater. I pulled her to the surface and hauled her back to the boat.

JD helped her over the transom. She had gotten a lungful of water and was hacking most of it out.

"I told you all to wear life preservers," JD said. "But nobody ever listens." JD shook his head. "I'd appreciate it if everybody would try to stay in the boat for the rest of the day."

The girl was pretty shaken up, and her girlfriends tried to console her. After a few minutes, it was business as usual, and the party restarted. But I noticed the little brat didn't go anywhere near the side of the boat.

When we docked at *Action Stations*, she couldn't get off the boat fast enough. I never saw her again after that. The redhead came back to tell us that they were going to stay at the bar and catch a cab back to their hotel on Coconut Key.

They gathered their belongings, and we were cut loose for the rest of the evening. That was fine by me and Jack. Once they had gotten all their gear, we cast off and headed back to *Diver Down*.

"How do you put up with this nonsense?" I asked.

"Oh, it's not that bad. Most of my clients are pretty cool. Now and then you get some rude ones." Jack grinned, "But like I said, the scenery's not bad."

15

That evening, JD and I decided to pay a visit to *Craig's Crab and Claw*. The restaurant was built in the shape of a large wooden boat. Fishing nets and classic signage hung from the walls. As the name suggested, they specialized in shellfish. The crab cakes were outstanding.

Jeremy's girlfriend, Catherine, was working, and we asked to be seated in her section. She greeted us with a friendly smile and didn't seem too broken up about recent events. "What can I get you to drink?"

She was mid-20s, had light brown, wavy hair, blue eyes and pale skin. She was the type who burned after 10 minutes in the sun. Despite living in a tropical paradise, she tried to avoid daylight as much as possible. And when she did go out, she slathered on the sunscreen. She was cute-ish. A little frumpy. And she wore her makeup extremely thick trying to cover the acne that was still left over from her teenage years. The braces she wore made her look younger than she was.

We ordered a couple of beers. When Catherine returned, she asked us if we'd had a chance to look over the menu. I decided it was time to get right to the point. "We'd like to talk to you about Jeremy?"

"What, are you guys cops? I already spoke with the sheriff earlier."

"We just have a few follow-up questions," I said. I didn't bother to tell her we weren't cops. No crime in that.

Her face tensed.

"Why don't you have a seat?" I suggested.

She hesitated, glanced around looking for her manager, then slid into the booth beside JD.

"When was the last time you saw Jeremy?" I asked.

"The morning he..." She couldn't finish the sentence. "I pulled a double here, so I was out of the house by 9 AM. We are open from 10 AM to 2 AM."

"So you closed here that night?" I asked.

Catherine nodded.

"What was your relationship like? Were you having any trouble?"

"I really don't see what that has to do with anything?"

"I know it's a difficult time, but this is really important."

Her alibi was easily verifiable. The restaurant was on the other side of the island from *Diver Down*. It's unlikely she could have snuck out during her shift, killed Jeremy, then made it back to serve the crab cakes.

"It's kind of embarrassing, but things were kind of rocky. I think he was fooling around on me."

"I'm sorry. Do you know with whom?"

"Yeah, that little blonde floozy who runs *Diver Down!*"

JD and I exchanged a doubtful glance. There was no way Jeremy was having a thing with my sister. She was way out of his league.

"Are you sure about that?" I asked.

"He spent damn near all his free time over there. I told him not to go over there again." Her eyes brimmed, tears rolled down her cheeks.

"How did that make you feel when he kept going over there?"

"Mad as hell."

"Mad enough to kill him?"

Her eyes sharpened as they flicked to me. "I didn't kill him. I loved that silly bastard."

The manager noticed his employee was in distress and he swung by the booth. "Is everything okay here?"

He was a thin man with wavy dark hair, dark eyes, and a thick unibrow that was in desperate need of tweezing.

"Yeah, it's fine," Catherine said, wiping her eyes. "These officers are just asking about Jeremy."

"She doesn't have to answer any of your questions without an attorney," the manager said.

"We're just trying to get to the bottom of things?" I said.

"It's okay," Catherine said. "I don't mind."

"Can I see some type of identification?" the manager asked.

JD pulled out his wallet and flashed what looked like an official ID. Most people don't know what law enforcement IDs actually look like. A confident flash of something remotely similar will usually do the trick.

The manager frowned, then reluctantly let us continue our interrogation.

"Did Jeremy have any enemies?" I asked.

Catherine shook her head. "He got along with everybody."

It was the Keys, so I had to ask, "What about drugs?"

"Jeremy never touched the stuff. All he did was drink. Maybe a little too much sometimes, but…"

"Did he owe anybody any money?" I asked, feeling like I was grasping at straws.

"Jeremy didn't have two nickels to rub together. He had to borrow money from me to pay rent this month."

"So, you two don't live together?"

"We had talked about it. And it would have saved us both money. It seems like he spent everything he had at *Diver Down*. Between that and his poker game, he was usually always scrounging for money. He wasn't working as much on the boat as he had been."

"Tell me about this poker game?" I asked. "Was it a game among friends? Or something else?"

JD gave me a look like he knew where this was going.

Catherine hesitated. "I'm not gonna get in trouble if I tell you something, am I?"

"No. You're not going to get in trouble," I assured.

16

"Tony Scarpetti? Are you sure?" JD asked.

"Yeah, that's what Jeremy said," Catherine replied.

I could tell by JD's look that something didn't fit. "What is it?"

"Scarpetti runs a big game," JD said.

"Like, how big?" I asked.

"$10,000 buy-in," JD replied.

Catherine's eyes went wide. "Jeremy didn't have that kind of money."

The manager glared at her, clearly frustrated that we had occupied a much-needed member of his waitstaff. The restaurant was pretty busy.

"I've got to get back to work. Please let me know what you find out."

"We will," I said as she slipped out of the booth.

JD had a grim look on his face.

"What's the deal with Scarpetti?"

"He's not a guy we want to cross. He's connected, if you know what I mean."

"I really don't care who he is," I said.

"I know. That's what bothers me."

"I think we should pay him a visit," I said.

"You certainly don't want to make it to old age, do you?" JD said, his voice thick with sarcasm.

"Not particularly. Have you been to an old folks' home recently? No way. Not for me. I want to get out clean."

"At the rate you're going, I have no doubt you will achieve your goal," JD said.

"I just need to stick around long enough to..."

"Long enough to what?"

I didn't feel like going into detail about my brush with the afterlife. "Nothing. Tell me about Scarpetti?"

"He's been running a high-stakes game for years. He's like a local institution. He runs a couple games a week. The cheapest buy-in is $10,000. If that's not rich enough for you, and you're someone special, you might get invited to his $100,000 by-in. His clients include celebrities, tech giants, you name it."

"That's highly illegal."

"Only if he takes a rake. He's been doing it long enough, I can guarantee you he's got people on the payroll."

"You mean like Sheriff Daniels?"

"And probably some feds. You don't move that kind of money without raising eyebrows."

"He sounds like the kind of guy who could have Jeremy killed."

"Sure. But no way Jeremy could buy his way into a game like that," Jack said.

"Maybe he saved his pennies?" I said.

JD shrugged. "Maybe he did." He sighed. "The question is, how many feathers do you want to ruffle to get to the bottom of this?"

I shrugged. "I've never been afraid of ruffling feathers. How do we get close to Scarpetti?"

"How good of a poker player are you?"

I grinned. I could hold my own.

We decided to indulge in the crab cakes and a few more beers. After we had our fill, JD drove me back to *Diver Down*. He sped away into the night, and I strolled into the bar. I asked Madison about her relationship with Jeremy one more time, and she denied any involvement.

Madison was anything but a liar.

We talked for a while, then I ambled down the dock to the *Slick'n Salty*. I still had to look over my shoulder. The cartel was still after me, and I was never able to totally let my guard down. I don't think I'll ever be able to completely relax. Situational awareness is part of the fabric of my being.

I climbed over the transom and pushed into the salon. I watched a little TV before crawling into bed and passing out. It wasn't like we had an exhausting day, but I was dead tired.

Jack called me the next morning and said, "Put on your poker face. I'm going to stake you in the next game."

"Can you afford that?"

"If you don't lose," he said. "And if you do, I know you're good for it."

"You've grown trusting in your old age."

"No. I just know how to pick horses."

I appreciated the confidence. Getting into the game would give us a look at Scarpetti's operation, and with any luck, I'd get a few words with Scarpetti. A man like that wouldn't talk about his business, but he might let something slip if I baited him well enough.

Bluffing my way through life and death situations was something I was quite familiar with. A poker game wasn't going to raise the needle on my blood pressure.

17

I fixed a pot of coffee, stepped into the cockpit, and took a deep breath of fresh air. The waves gently lapped against the hull of the boat, and the warm rays of morning sun hit my face. From the corner of my eye, I caught a glance of something I didn't expect.

The bratty brunette from the charter sauntered down the dock. She wore a blue bikini top that hugged her all natural endowments, frayed jean shorts, and a pair of designer *Steve Madden* sneakers. The breeze blew her hair perfectly, like this was a fashion photo shoot. The dock was her catwalk.

I cringed.

She was probably going to complain about the service, or demand payment for the phone.

As she reached the back of the transom, she pulled down her sunglasses, revealing beautiful blue eyes. With a bright smile she said, "Good morning."

"Good morning," I responded, hesitantly.

"You're still mad at me, aren't you?" She had a sheepish tone.

"Why would I be mad at you?" I said with a trace of sarcasm.

"Well, I was kind of a bitch to you," she said, cringing.

I could tell she was embarrassed. She waited for my response, but I was hesitant to speak my mind.

"You don't have to pretend I wasn't. I had too much to drink, and I was acting like a spoiled brat. I'm sorry."

Usually I disregard apologies. For the most part, they're meaningless. People just say *I'm sorry* to make themselves feel better and to stay on amicable terms so that when they need something from you later they can ask.

But then she did something I didn't expect.

She added the only thing that can make an apology valid— an offer to make things right. "What can I do to make it up to you?"

It was said with innocent intentions. She wasn't throwing herself at me or offering sexual favors. It seemed like she genuinely wanted to atone for her sins.

I thought about it for a moment. "You just made it up to me. I owe you an apology as well. I overreacted. I shouldn't have thrown your phone in the water. I'll buy you a new one."

She smiled. "I got another one." She pulled it out and displayed it, then slipped it into her back pocket. "Besides, you saved my life. That's worth a hell of a lot more than a phone."

She paused for a minute, pondering the situation. A mischievous grin tugged at her luscious lips. "Me and my friends are flying back to New York tomorrow. How about I take you to breakfast?"

"That's not necessary," I said, regretting the statement the minute it slipped from my mouth. This girl was adorably cute.

"Oh, come on. It's the least I can do."

I sighed, as if sitting across the table from her would be torture. "Okay. I *guess* I can let you take me to breakfast."

A bright smile flashed on her face. She bounced slightly as she cheered, "Yay!"

My eyes couldn't help but be drawn to her jiggling...

I turned toward the deck house. "Let me put on a shirt and I'll be right out."

"Shirtless is fine by me," she said. She bit her lip and ogled me as I slipped into the salon.

I felt like a piece of meat. It felt good.

I didn't bother grabbing my pistol. I didn't think I'd need it. That was a mistake.

I pulled on a T-shirt, scurried through the boat, climbed the transom, and escorted the beautiful brunette down the dock. We caught an Uber over to Ziggy's. The restaurant was known for their breakfast, and you could get it all hours of the day and night.

Ziggy's was a patio restaurant ensconced by palm trees. They offered vegetarian and gluten-free entrées as well as regular fair. A guy with a guitar strummed Bob Marley songs. It was never to early to order a Margarita. If you weren't in the mood for breakfast, they had barbecued shrimp, Jamaican jerked chicken, beef tenderloin, and an assortment of seafood items. I went for the French toast, bacon, and hash browns. My stunning companion ordered blueberry waffles, fresh fruit, and scrambled eggs.

We got reacquainted with one another, this time under better circumstances. She told me her name was Aria. I'm sure she had mentioned it when I first met her on the boat, but it went in one ear and out the other.

She took a picture of her breakfast when it was served. It looked appetizing, and the presentation was perfect. She posted it to her followers and had a thousand likes within a few seconds.

"JD says you're some type of Internet celebrity?"

She rolled her eyes. "I guess. Whatever that means."

"How does that work?"

She shrugged. "I just post pictures of me and my friends on fabulous vacations and at exclusive parties. I mean, you've seen my friends, they're hot. Companies pay me to wear their bikinis and their lingerie and post about it. I do traditional modeling jobs as well."

"So, let me get this straight. Companies *pay* you to go on vacation and post a few pics?"

"Yeah, pretty much."

"I don't want to ask... but it obviously pays well."

Her eyes grew big. "Very."

"Sounds like a sweet gig if you can get it."

"It's not something I planned for. I was going to go to med school, but then this whole modeling thing took off, and, well, here I am." She smiled. "What about you? I'm sorry I got you fired. But it looks like you got your job back, right?" She said, hopeful.

I hesitated. I always hated lying to people, but I couldn't exactly tell them I was a covert agent. "Yes, I got my job back. JD and I are old friends. So, I'm helping him out on the boat while I get situated."

"It seems like a fun job... when you don't have to put up with spoiled brats," she said with a wry smile.

There was a moment of silence between us.

"So, what's your dream job? If you could do anything in the world you wanted to do, what would it be?" she asked.

The only thing I wanted to do was redeem myself. I needed to leave the world a better place than I found it, even if it was for selfish reasons. I had no intention of going back to hell. "I don't know. I'm still trying to figure that out. I just want to make a difference."

"Me too. I don't know if posting pictures of me wearing a bikini is making a difference, but maybe someday I'll do something meaningful."

"I don't know. I'm sure your bikini photos are bringing joy to millions of men."

"Are you saying you like the way I look in a bikini?"

"Maybe," I said, teasing her.

We finished breakfast and caught a ride back to the Marina. We exchanged numbers, and she kissed me on the cheek and told me to look her up if I ever found myself in New York. I figured I would never see her again, but it was a hell of a way to start off the day.

I strolled down the dock with a little extra pep in my step, fantasizing about things that might have been. I hadn't enjoyed a nice breakfast with a woman in a long time, and it reminded me that I was still alive, and that life could be worth living.

I was so preoccupied with my thoughts that I didn't pay much attention to the guy with a fillet knife in the cockpit of the *Ships & Giggles*. He had his back turned toward me, fiddling with something in the bait prep area. An instant after I passed by, he leapt over the transom and attacked.

18

The metal blade glimmered in the sunlight as he stabbed at me. I had sensed him behind me and spun around in time to deflect the strike.

I blocked his forearm and grabbed his wrist. With my free hand I jammed his elbow toward the sky, twisting his arm. At the same time I bent his wrist well past the point of pain.

The knife fell from his grasp and clattered against the deck. I kicked it into the water. It plunked through the surface and sank to the depths.

In a continuous motion, I did an arm-bar take down. Bones cracked. I dropped down, planting my knee in his back and twisted his arm even farther.

The man groaned in agony.

Gang tattoos extended beyond his collar.

"Who sent you?" I didn't need to ask. He was from the cartel.

He didn't respond, so I twisted his arm again. I heard more pops and crackles. He screamed again.

I frisked him as best I could and found another pocketknife, which I tossed into the water. He had a cell phone, and I told him to call his employer and tell them the hit had been completed.

He was reluctant at first. But with a little subtle persuasion, he agreed. He didn't have much choice. The old me would have snapped his neck and neutralized the threat. But I was trying to scale back my use of lethal force to situations that were absolutely necessary.

I don't know who the man called. He could have been calling his uncle for all I knew. But I had put the fear of God into him. I could hear the other man's voice filter through the tiny speaker in the cell phone. He sounded pleased that the job had been accomplished and hung up the phone.

This is when I would have killed the man. Instead I used his cell phone to dial 911. I held him on the dock until the deputy sheriff showed up and arrested the man.

I told Deputy Perkins that the gang member attacked me, probably trying to steal my wallet. By this time, a crowd had gathered on the dock. Perkins slapped the cuffs on him and carted him away, and the crowd erupted with cheers.

The man would probably spend the next few days in the county jail. It wouldn't take them long to determine he was undocumented. They'd send him back where he came from, and his employers wouldn't be happy to find out he had lied about completing the job.

There was no doubt I hadn't seen the last of the cartel.

Madison ran to me with worried eyes and gave me a hug. "Are you okay? What happened?"

I was surprised to see so much concern from her. I think she was a little surprised by her reaction as well. "I'm fine. The guy was a moron. He picked a fight he couldn't win."

"Do you think that's the guy who killed Jeremy?"

"No. I seriously doubt he would confuse the two of us."

Suspicion narrowed her eyes. "What do you mean *confuse the two of you?*"

I realized I had put my foot in my mouth. "I mean, he was confused if he thought he could take me down."

Madison didn't buy my response. "What's going on here?"

"I don't think these two attacks are related."

"A guy tries to mug you on the dock. Jeremy is killed by the dumpster, and his watch was stolen. You don't think the two are related?"

"No. I don't."

"Why not?" she said in a stern tone.

"Can we talk about this later?"

"No, we can't talk about this later."

The crowd was starting to dissipate, but they were still within earshot. I suggested we continue this conversation in private. We boarded the *Slick'n Salty*, and I offered Madison a seat at the lounge.

"Do you want a beer?"

"No. I don't want a beer. I want you to tell me what's going on!"

I moved to the galley and grabbed a beer from the fridge, then sat at the dinette. I twisted the cap off the longneck and the compressed air rushed free. I took a long pull and thought about how I was going to position this. This whole *truth* thing was new to me, but I figured it was time to come clean. "I didn't want to alarm you."

"I'm alarmed." Her eyes were wide, and her intense gaze demanded answers.

"There's a lot you don't know about my life."

"That's because you keep your cards close to your chest."

"It's safer for everybody that way."

She rolled her eyes. "You may think you're keeping the people around you safe with all this cloak and dagger shit. But as evidenced by recent events, it's not working."

I caught her up to speed on everything that had happened since Mexico. The expression on her face was a mix of horror, shock, and rage.

"I came back because I wanted to be able to keep you safe," I said.

"I don't think you're doing a very good job of it. Jeremy could be dead because of you."

"I really don't think they are connected."

"But you don't know that for sure." She looked like she was about to explode. She grumbled to herself and clenched her fists. "You should never have come back here."

19

M adison stormed off the boat.

I ran a frustrated hand through my hair and sighed. I was trying to fix my relationship with my sister, and I had made it worse.

I called JD and told him what happened. He swung by that afternoon and picked me up. He decided it was best if I improved my attire before the poker game. Most multi-millionaires I knew were rather unassuming individuals. They weren't terribly flashy and didn't like to attract attention to themselves.

Still, cargo shorts and a T-shirt didn't exude wealth.

We drove to Highland Village and shopped at several high-end boutiques. I picked up a nice *Zangari* cream colored linen suit, a blue cotton broadcloth shirt by *Bonaccorso*, a blue silk pocket square by *Boveri*, and leather loafers by *Agnellini*.

The whole ensemble set me back $1,699. Or I should say, set

JD back. He fronted the whole thing. It was a little much if you ask me. "I feel ridiculous."

"You look great. Definite high roller."

"Jeremy wasn't a high roller."

"Trust me. You want to make Scarpetti feel at ease. If he thinks you will be an easy mark that has a lot of money to spend, he might open up a little. Besides, if you don't get blood on the suit, we might be able to take it back. I know a girl who can put tags back on."

"What about the shoes?"

"At $600 a pair, we can afford to have them re-soled. Then return them for new."

I shook my head. JD always had an angle.

He payed cash for everything, then we grabbed an early dinner at *Blowfish*. It was an upscale sushi joint—the best on the island. The stunning waitresses wore skintight bodysuits with low-cut necklines and black fishnet stockings.

It was a feast for both the eyes and the belly.

Their premier dish, and namesake, was the Japanese fugu fish—a lethal puffer fish that contained tetrodotoxin, which required special preparation to remove the deadly portion of the meat.

I didn't need to tempt fate. I had already had enough near-death experiences. The salmon and a California roll would do me just fine.

I talked Jack out of the puffer fish, and instead he ordered edamame, a spicy tuna roll, ootoro, a Kirin Light, and sake.

I decided not to drink since I needed to be on my A-game.

Jack couldn't keep his eyes off the waitresses. "I think the next ex-Mrs. Donovan might be wandering around this place."

"The last thing you need is another ex-wife."

"When are you going to settle down, start building a family?"

I looked at him like he was crazy. "When people stop trying to kill me."

"At that rate, you're going to be single for a long time."

"If people would just take the time to get to know me, they might not want to kill me," I said in a dry tone.

"I don't know," Jack said, doubtful. "Your sister knows you pretty well, and I think she's about ready to kill you."

"She is not a happy camper. I don't blame her. The last thing I wanted was to drag her into my lifestyle."

"Jeremy is not your fault. And this guy today... well, maybe that's your fault. But, in your defense, you eliminated the threat quickly and without incident."

"Yeah, but what about next time?"

JD thought about this for a moment. "Just don't get any bullet holes in my boat."

I frowned at him.

Our waitress stopped by to check on us. "Is there anything else I can get for you?"

I could see the lewd comment brewing behind JD's eyes, but

he restrained himself. The waitress was gorgeous—raven black hair, pale skin, red lips, fishnet stockings.

"Just the check please," JD said.

She started away, then turned back. "I hope you don't mind, but I was wondering if you could settle a bet?"

JD grinned. He knew what was coming next.

"Honey, I'd be happy to do anything you need me to do."

She giggled. "My friend says you're famous. She bet 20 bucks that you're the lead singer of this '80s band... *Molly Who?* Or something like that."

She'd never heard of the band and wasn't born yet when they were topping the charts. It made both JD and I feel old.

Under normal circumstances, Jack would have assumed his alter ego and let everyone believe he was a celebrity. But I could tell he didn't want our waitress to lose the bet.

"I hate to disappoint, but I'm not famous."

The waitress smiled and pulled a fist in celebration. "You just made me twenty bucks!"

"In that case, do I still need to leave a tip?"

She squinted at him. "Yes, of course you do."

"Don't worry. The service was outstanding."

She flashed a cutesy smile and kicked up her heel like Betty Boop. "Thank you."

She returned a few minutes later with our tab, and JD peeled off a wad of bills. "Keep the change."

Her eyes widened at the hundred dollar tip. "This is turning out to be a good night. Thank you."

She cleared our plates and sauntered away.

Jack grabbed the receipt from the table and was about to stuff it in his pocket when he looked it over. "Well, would you look at that?"

He showed me the paper. The waitress had written her number on the receipt.

Jack grinned. "The next ex-Mrs. Donovan?"

20

Jack handed me a fat roll of cash when we got back into his car. And when I say fat, I mean fat. $10,000 in crisp hundreds, rolled up and bound by a rubber band.

"Big pimp'n," I said.

"You know it."

We drove to the *Seven Seas Hotel*. It was a luxury five-star resort. The valet took the car, and we strolled through the opulent lobby. The hotel was centered around a spectacular pool that faced the ocean. There was a private marina and a small private shell beach. We took the glass elevator up to the third floor. I knocked on #319 and a thick meathead wearing a dark suit pulled open the door. I instantly took notice of the .45 that was tucked under his armpit in a shoulder holster. I flashed the wad of cash and he motioned for us to enter.

The furniture inside the suite had been replaced with a poker table. There was a fully stocked bar, and two gorgeous blondes in tight cocktail dresses served as much as you liked. Just like Vegas, the drinks were free. Scarpetti was there to oversee the game.

The game hadn't started yet, and several would-be players mingled about the suite, drinking and talking to the girls. There was an investment banker from Wall Street, a dentist from Colorado, a tech guru from Silicon Valley, an ad exec from Los Angeles, a cattle rancher from Texas, and a mortician from Georgia. Several others came and went during the night.

I traded my cash for game checks and sat at the table. No limit Texas hold 'em. I wasn't a beginner, but I wasn't a pro.

The small and big blinds were posted, and the cards were dealt. My first hand was a disappointment—7 of Clubs, and a 2 of Diamonds. I folded before the flop. If the whole night was going to be like this, I was in for trouble.

The next round wasn't much better. 2 of Clubs, 6 of Spades. Even if the stars aligned, and the flop was 3, 4, and 5, the odds that someone had a 6 and 7 were high.

I folded.

I kept getting these crappy starting cards. I thought I was cursed. I hadn't lost anything except for the occasional blind bid as the deal rotated around the table.

Then something changed.

Cigar smoke filled the air, and chips clacked as players fidgeted with stacks. Ice cubes rattled in drink glasses.

A pair of aces came my way. That kicked off a streak that

was so hot, even I would have thought I was cheating. In an hour, I was up $127,000.

That's when I probably should have quit. It would have been the smart thing to do. But I was here to gather information—not win a pile of money. Although that would have been a welcomed bonus.

I had a bad feeling that my luck was about to run out. Call it gut instinct.

I got dealt a 10, 8, off suit.

The pot was $23,500 before the flop.

The flop—8, 8, Queen.

Wall Street, Tex, and the Mortician folded.

Everybody checked at the turn.

Deuce of Clubs.

The Dentist looked confident. He raised $8,000.

I re-raised $40,000.

Tech Giant called at $40,000.

The River came down—another 8.

Mortician folded.

I went all in at $85,000. I had to admit, my BP might have been a little elevated.

The tech giant called.

That brought the pot to $281,500.

The Tech Giant only had a king and a queen.

I tried to contain my joy as I scooped up my winnings. The tech giant didn't seem fazed at the loss.

It was definitely time for me to get out of there. I pushed away from the table and went to cash out my chips. I barely had enough pockets to stuff in all the cash.

Scarpetti approached and put a hand on my shoulder. He was a big man, late 40s, dark hair, hard face. He had a few scars around his eyebrows from street fights, no doubt. Clearly a New York mafia guy. "You had a good night."

I shrugged, innocently. "The cards fell my way."

"Why don't you come with me?"

He gently ushered me into the next room. One of his bodyguards followed.

I had hoped to draw his attention by playing flashy and making big bets. It seemed like my strategy worked. I only hoped this wasn't the part where I got worked over with a lead pipe.

I couldn't tell exactly what was behind his eyes. Scarpetti took a rake from every pot. As far as he was concerned, it didn't matter who walked away with the money at the end of the night. He got his cut.

"We always like new players," Scarpetti said. "A player of your caliber might enjoy something more exclusive."

"More exclusive?"

"I run another, invite only, game. $100,000 buy-in. Seems like that might be right up your alley?"

"I'm intrigued."

"Third Tuesday of the month. Same place. Feel free to stop by anytime. Congratulations on your winnings." He turned toward the door, then stopped. "By the way, how did you find out about the game?"

"Jeremy Phelps."

I saw the recognition in Scarpetti's eyes. "Good friend of yours?"

"No. Not really. We met in a bar. Got to talking. We both had poker in common. It's a shame what happened to him."

"Yes. It is." The muscles in Scarpetti's jaw flexed. He was angry about it.

"This game seems a little out of his league," I said.

"It was way out of his league," Scarpetti said. "But, let's just say I was friendly with the kid's mother. He did okay for a little while. Then he got upside down. I covered a few of his bets. He owed the house about $150,000. The way I see it, whoever killed him stole from me. And nobody steals from me."

21

"That pretty much rules Scarpetti out," Jack said.

The valet pulled JD's Porsche around, and we climbed in. The flat six howled as Jack dropped it into gear and sped away. I pulled out a couple stacks of cash from my pocket and offered them to JD. "Here's $10,000 for the stake, plus a couple grand for the outfit, and a little extra for the effort."

His face contorted. "You are out of your goddamn mind. That's a 50-50 split, son. You wouldn't have had the game, or the cash if it weren't for me."

"50%?" I said with raised eyebrows.

"Damn skippy! I took all the risk. I share in the reward."

"Fine. You drive a hard bargain, Jack."

"Plus, now you can start paying rent." He flashed a miserly grin.

"There's no way Scarpetti killed Jeremy while he had an outstanding debt," I said.

"Maybe he sent someone to scare him and things went wrong?"

"No. I think he had a soft spot for the kid."

We drove back to *Diver Down* and divvied up the cash in the parking lot. Despite giving JD his cut, I still walked with $137,750. Not a bad night's haul.

I told Jack I'd touch base with him in the morning, and he sped away into the night. I stepped into the bar and settled my tab with Madison. Her suspicious eyes surveyed me and the money. "What did you do? Rob a bank?"

"Lady Luck smiled on me."

"So, you've taken up gambling now? That's great," she said, her voice thick with sarcasm.

"My whole life has been a gamble."

I had a few beers before heading back to the marina. As I stepped out of the bar, I was greeted with a crowbar to the belly.

My stomach leapt into my throat. I doubled over with pain, then felt the sharp break of the crowbar against my back. The impact flattened me against the deck. The wood smelled like a mixture of stale beer and bleach.

A voice said, "Quit nosing around. Things could get dangerous for you and your sister."

I didn't see the man's face. He wore a ski mask, and he disappeared before I could draw my weapon. He didn't bother to look in my pockets, or he would have found a nice windfall.

I pushed off the ground and staggered back into the bar. My belly ached, and my back was already black and blue. It was going to be sore as hell in the morning.

"Close the bar," I said to Madison. "Pack your things. You're leaving tonight."

She looked at me like I was crazy. "We had this conversation. I think you're the one who should probably go."

"It wasn't a suggestion. Do it. Now!"

"I am not gonna let you come in here and boss me around. You signed away your rights to this bar a long time ago."

"Madison, you don't understand. Whoever killed Jeremy just attacked me and threatened you."

Her face crinkled, perplexed. "What?"

I lifted my shirt to reveal the welt across my stomach and back. "Somebody just took a crowbar to me."

Her eyes widened with horror.

"Now please, cose this place down, pack a bag, and go stay with one of your model friends in South Beach."

She stammered, "Uh, yeah. Okay."

I started closing and locking the bay doors. Madison shouted, "Alright. Bar's closed. You don't have to go home, but you can't stay here!"

There were groans among the patrons—it was well before closing time.

After we got the bar cleaned up, and the staff left, Madison gathered her belongings. She lived in a loft apartment above the bar. She packed a small suitcase, and I helped her load it into her Jeep.

"What are you going to do?" She asked, sitting in the driver seat. The top was down, and the cool breeze ruffled her blonde hair.

"I'm going to get to the bottom of this. I'll call you when it's safe to come back."

"What if you don't find who did this? I can't stay gone forever. I've worked too hard to keep this bar going, and I'm barely getting by as it is. It's all I have left of Mom and Dad."

"Don't worry about that."

"I'm worried."

"I've got enough to float you for a little while."

"If it stays closed for too long, people will find someplace else to go. And they won't come back. People get in habits."

"I promise, I'll figure this out soon. I'm getting close." I wasn't getting close at all. I had nothing.

"I'll call you when I get to Hannah's," she said. Then she added, "Be careful."

"You too. Tell Hannah I said hello."

Madison nodded. She started the engine, dropped the car into gear, and sped away. The tires spit loose gravel as she turned onto the highway. I watched the yellow Jeep disappear into the night, her blonde hair flapping in the breeze.

The parking lot was empty now, bathed in the amber glow

of a vapor light overhead. I ambled back to the marina and strolled down the dock to the *Slick'n Salty*. I stashed my winnings in the storage compartment under the master bed. Then I found some arnica gel and slathered it on my bruises. I don't know if it was the placebo effect, but it had always worked wonders for sore muscles in the past.

I climbed into bed and tried to get some sleep. My mind was still racing from the evening's events. Too much adrenaline coursing through my veins. I lay there staring at the roof deck for what seemed like an hour, listening to the waves lap against the hull. It was sometime after 2 AM when I heard what I thought were footsteps in the cockpit.

Probably just my overactive imagination.

Then I heard the hatch to the deck house creak open. There was no mistaking it.

I grabbed my pistol from underneath the pillow and launched out of bed. My feet quietly hit the deck, and I inched toward the hatch of the master stateroom with my weapon in the firing position, ready to blast at the intruder.

22

I burst through the hatch and stepped into the salon. It was a good thing I didn't pull the trigger.

Aria tiptoed through the salon in bare feet, holding her stiletto heels. She wore a skimpy little dress that hugged her perfect form. She shrieked in terror when she saw the gun and dropped the heels. They clacked against the deck like a gunshot.

I lowered my weapon instantly. "Sorry, I thought you were an intruder."

"You always pull a gun on your guests?"

"I wasn't expecting company. What are you doing here?"

"I can leave if this is a bad time."

"No. This isn't a bad time." I learned a few things in life, one of them is not to turn away a beautiful woman in the middle of the night.

She smiled. "Good."

I flipped on a light, and she squinted from the brightness.

"I was out with my girlfriends, and since we are leaving in the morning, I had them drop me off here," she said with a naughty grin. "I hope you don't mind."

"No. Not at all."

There was a long pause.

Her eyes finally focused on my bruised abdomen. "Oh, my God, what happened?"

She moved toward me and reached out a delicate hand.

"Nothing. Small altercation with a crowbar."

"Does it hurt?"

I grabbed her hand before she touched my bruise. "A little."

We were inches apart. I could feel her body heat, and her warm breath on my chest. The sexual tension between us was palpable.

"I can kiss it and make it better," she said in an innocent voice that made the rational, logical part of my brain shut down.

She leaned in and gently pressed her full lips against my abdomen. She traced her tongue down well past the bruise. She dropped to her knees and grabbed the waistband of my boxers.

The girl was talented. No doubt about it. We explored every available surface of the salon, then finally ended up in the stateroom.

I was a wounded warrior, but believe me, I pushed through the pain of my recent injuries.

The morning came too soon. I didn't want the night to end. I got up, made a pot of coffee, and started scrambling eggs and frying bacon.

There was a text from Madison saying she had reached Miami safely and was staying with Hannah. I felt relieved. She said she had called Alejandro, and he would be opening the bar and running it while she was gone. She wasn't about to let business go down the toilet.

I fixed a plate for Aria and brought it into the stateroom. I hated to wake her. She looked so perfect sleeping naked in my bed, but I knew she had to catch a flight back to New York. I set the breakfast tray down and gently nudged her. "Wake up, sleepyhead."

She stretched and yawned and rolled over. Her gorgeous eyes peeled open, and she looked just as beautiful in the morning as she did the night before. "I made breakfast."

"Yay!" she said, perking up.

She grabbed a slice of bacon and crunched it.

"What time is your flight?"

"What time is it now?"

I looked at my watch—it was 9 AM.

"Shit! I gotta go. Our flight leaves at 10:30."

She finished the slice of bacon and shoveled in a few mouthfuls of scrambled eggs, then climbed out of bed and got dressed. She wrapped her arms around me and squeezed tight enough that the bruises hurt, but I didn't say anything. She gave me a long kiss, then said, "I hate to run out like this. I had a really good time."

"So did I."

There was a long awkward silence between us. It was a one-night stand, and we both knew it. There wasn't any sense dressing it up as something it wasn't. But there no denying we had chemistry between us.

"You should really come see me in New York sometime."

"I will." I meant it when I said it. But, you know how things are. Life happens, and I would probably never see her again.

"Promise?"

"Promise."

"You're just saying that."

"No. I'd really like to see you again."

"Me too." She looked around the stateroom, but didn't find what she was looking for. She shyly asked, "Do you know where my panties are?"

"I think they're in the salon."

Sure enough, they were on the deck by the lounge. She slipped them on, pulling them up her toned legs. Then she shimmied her skirt back down over her hips. She gave me a last kiss on the lips before she ran out of the deck house barefoot, clinging onto her stilettos. "I'll let you know when I touch down in New York."

"Please do. Safe journey."

23

I finished breakfast and crawled back into bed. I could still smell her on my pillow—the strawberry shampoo, a trace of perfume. I breathed her in. The place seemed so empty without her. It had been ages since I'd had an overnight guest. I'd almost forgotten what it was like. I couldn't help but feel a little deflated knowing she wasn't coming back.

In my line of work, you get used to walking away from things. It doesn't matter if there are close connections or not. Sometimes it's easy to walk away, sometimes it's not. But there comes a time in life when you realize you can't keep walking away from things forever.

I tried to look on the bright side. At least we had one good night. Life's about the journey, not the destination.

I took a deep breath and refocused my mind. I had some assholes to track down. It wasn't just about Jeremy anymore. They were threatening me and my family.

JD called. "Morning, sunshine. I have interesting news."

"I bet my news is more interesting."

"I don't know about that. This is pretty juicy."

I told him about my encounter with Aria, and with the crowbar.

"I want details. Leave nothing out," JD said.

"About Aria, or about my attacker?"

"Both," he said.

"Later. Let's hear your news first."

"Got the ME's report. The murder weapon was most likely a 7-inch fillet knife. There were multiple cut marks in the bone on the 6th, 7th, and 8th ribs, as well as the 2nd and 3rd cervical vertebrae."

"Great. Do you know how many filet knives there are in the area?"

"Wait for it. Here's the kicker. The blade had a titanium nitride coating. When the blade made contact with the bone, it left microscopic flakes of the coating. Brenda sent them to the FBI crime lab for analysis. Turns out, it's a commercial variant, the formula is proprietary to one specific manufacturer."

"Now you're talking. Which brand?"

"Krüger-Schmidt."

My eyes widened. "I saw one of those recently."

"Should I hazard a guess where?"

JD swung by the marina, and we headed to Pirates' Cove. It was time to pay Dan Baker another visit. The fillet knife I had seen in his bait prep area was a Krüger-Schmidt. They were rare, expensive, and had a distinctive blue handle and black blade. There was no mistaking one.

At the marina, we moved down the dock toward Dan's boat, the *Heartbreaker*. It was sunny and warm, and the sky was crystal clear. I was surprised not to see anyone prepping the boat.

"Dan? You in there?" JD shouted.

There was no response.

The hatch to the deckhouse was slightly ajar. We glanced around the area, looking for Dan or any of his deckhands, but the dock was empty.

"It would be unlikely he'd leave his hatch unlocked," JD said.

We climbed over the transom and pushed open the hatch. What we saw in the salon was disturbing.

Dan lay face down on the deck in a pool of blood.

I drew my weapon out of instinct. The killer could have been close by. I started to step into the deckhouse, but JD put a hand on my arm. "Don't go traipsing around. The last thing we need is Sheriff Daniels breathing down our neck."

He was right. I didn't want to contaminate the area. The last thing I needed were my bloody footprints on Dan's boat. "Looks like blunt force trauma to me."

The back of Dan's hair was matted with crusted blood. He'd

been struck in the back of the head with an object. Blood had trickled down his cheek and pooled around his face. There was no doubt he had a subdural hematoma from the trauma. The swelling and intracranial pressure probably caused his death.

JD snapped a few pictures with his cell phone, then zoomed in to get a better look. We focused on the wound to the back of Dan's scalp.

"I don't know about you, but that looks like it could have been caused by a crowbar," JD said.

I agreed.

Jack dialed 911, and before long the marina was buzzing with investigators and local media. Yellow tape blocked off the area, and the forensics team went to work.

Brenda Sparks gave a nervous glance to JD when he arrived. She'd lose her job if it got out she shared her report with him. He never told me what he had to do to bribe her, but I had my suspicions.

Sheriff Daniels was not happy to see us. "You want to tell me what the hell you two are doing here?"

"I needed Dan to take over a charter for me and I wanted to see if he had any space available," Jack said.

Brenda was in earshot and she seemed relieved by Jack's story.

Sheriff Daniels's doubtful eyes glared at us. "You two have a funny way of stumbling across murder victims."

"Just lucky, I guess," I said in monotone.

"Have either of you clowns contaminated my crime scene?"

"No, sir," I said.

"So you haven't stepped aboard that boat?"

"We were in the cockpit, and you'll find my fingerprints on the hatch. Once we saw the body, we called you."

"If I find anything in that deckhouse that ties this crime to you, I'll nail your ass to the wall."

We did our best to look innocent.

"When did you find the body?" the sheriff asked.

"When I called 911," JD said. "11:30-ish? You can check the call logs to verify that."

"You don't need to tell me how to do my job." The sheriff glared at us both. He called over his shoulder to Brenda who was in the salon examining the body. "You got a time of death yet?"

"He's pretty fresh. I put it about 8:30am or 9, give or take."

Sheriff Daniels's suspicious eyes glanced back to me. He just wanted to arrest me for something. Anything. I could see it in his eyes. "I suppose you've got an alibi?"

"I do. But you're barking up the wrong tree. I didn't kill Dan Baker. What possible motive would I have?"

The sheriff shrugged. "Tell me about this alibi."

"Brunette, 5'5", great..." I cupped my hands in front of my chest, "eyes."

"I'm going to need her information. Where is she now?"

"On her way back to New York."

He sneered at me and turned his gaze to JD. "What about you?"

"Cut the crap, Wayne. You know neither one of us had anything to do with this."

"Just answer the goddamn question."

"I was at home, cooking my daughter breakfast."

Sheriff Daniels wrote the information down in his little notebook.

"You're going to interview his deckhands, aren't you?" I asked.

Sheriff Daniels took a deep breath and tried not to explode. "I will interview anyone I think is relevant to this case. And yes, they are high on my list." He paused. "All of Dan's fishing rods are missing, and someone took a crowbar and pried out the stereo on the bridge. If you ask me, I think Dan startled a burglar, and they whacked him over the head."

"You don't think this is related to Jeremy's death?" I asked, incredulous.

The sheriff shrugged. "I don't know yet. But I don't think so. Two different weapons. Two different MOs. One was a mugging in a parking lot, the other was a B&E."

"First a deckhand is murdered, then his skipper. And you don't think they're connected?" I bit my tongue for a moment. "And what about the guy who attacked me with a crowbar and told me to stop snooping around?" I asked.

"You were assaulted?" Sheriff Daniels asked, surprised. "Why didn't you report it?"

I shrugged. Then I said, smugly, "I didn't think it would do much good."

Wayne took it as it was meant—a subtle jab at his law enforcement skills.

"If you've got something to say to me, just say it," Sheriff Daniels said.

I shrugged again.

His body tensed and he let out a long exhale. "I didn't know your parents well. I moved here shortly before they disappeared. I want you to know that I did everything I could to track down your parents' killers. And I know you think I've been sitting around on my ass, but there's not a day that goes by that I don't think about them. There wasn't much to go on. Their bodies had been out to sea for weeks before they washed up on shore. By that time, there was almost no useable evidence. We recovered a couple slugs, but the FBI wasn't able to match ballistics to anything in their database."

There was a long, uncomfortable moment of silence.

"I know. I had a friend at the Bureau look into it," I said.

Sheriff Daniels seemed surprised I had contacts at the FBI.

"He's pretty well connected," JD said. "Or at least, he used to be."

"I pulled your file," Daniels said. "There's not much in there. At least, not much I can access. Says you graduated from Vanden University as a EE major, then worked for a multinational energy corporation, DynaCorp Global LTD. Then supposedly had a job as a private energy consultant. That just doesn't add up to me. 15 minutes after I ran your background check, I got a call from both the FBI and the CIA. You want to tell me what your story is? Cause I can't tell if you're a criminal, or one of the good guys?"

24

"He's one of the good guys," JD assured.

"I couldn't get either agency to give me any additional information," Sheriff Daniels said. "They just wanted to know where you were, and what you were up to?"

I didn't say anything.

"Something tells me you're not back in the Keys doing energy consulting," Daniels added.

He stared at me for a moment, then sighed, "Well, in all your snooping, have you found anything useful?"

"Not much, I'm afraid," I said. "The guy that assaulted me was Caucasian, 6'1", 220 pounds."

"Did you get a look at his face?" the sheriff asked.

"He wore a ski mask. Caught me off guard."

"So what made you two come out here and check on Dan?"

JD and I exchanged a glance.

"Call it a hunch," I said.

There was another long pause as Sheriff Daniels sized me up. "I had occasion to speak with your father a few times before he died. I like to get out and meet the community. He invited me in and offered a cup of coffee. We got to talking, and he mentioned you had done some time in the Navy. Showed me a picture. But your service record is not in your file."

He waited for me to say something, but I didn't.

"I don't know anybody who can make their military history go away. If you had gotten a dishonorable discharge, that would stay on your permanent record."

"I didn't get a dishonorable discharge, I can assure you of that."

"As far as I can figure, the only way your file could be altered was if it was done by the government. Now, I may not be a rocket scientist, but I'd wager you are either some kind of clandestine operative, or in the witness relocation program. Which one is it?"

I paused for a moment. I'd always abided by the philosophy of *never admit anything and deny till death*. But we weren't going to get any help from Sheriff Daniels unless he felt he could trust us. "I can tell you this... I'm not in the witness relocation program. That's all I can say about that."

He thought about it for a moment. "Fair enough. Like I said, I didn't know your father well, but he seemed like a good man. The apple can't fall too far from the tree, I suppose."

"I don't think this one fell far at all," JD said.

"I probably shouldn't be telling you this, but we found microscopic particles of a titanium nitride coating from the murder weapon in the first victim," Sheriff Daniels said.

We tried to act like it was the first time we heard the information.

"Dan had the same brand of fillet knife," Sheriff Daniels continued. "I recalled seeing it when I was out here the other day. I was planning on paying him a visit today, then your call came in."

"Still think this was a robbery gone wrong?" Jack asked in a sardonic tone.

"No. I don't."

"I think we need to talk to Dan's first mate, Luke..." I didn't know his last name.

"Luke Meyer. He's been with Dan for a few years. But I can guarantee you he didn't do this."

"How can you be so certain?" I asked.

"Because we picked him up last night on a DUI. He's still in the tank."

I deflated. It didn't seem like we had any other leads.

"We can talk to his other deckhands," the sheriff added.

My eyes perked up. "Deckhands?"

"Garrett Hardin and Troy Larson."

"We only met his first mate Luke the other day," I said.

Sheriff Daniels thought for a moment. "Come to think of it... Troy Larson matches the description of your assailant. He's about 6'1", 220 pounds."

"I never saw his face," I said. "But I heard his voice."

"Think you'd recognize it if you heard it again?" the sheriff asked.

"Yeah."

"I don't think that's enough to make anything stick. A defense attorney would tear it apart. But at least we'd know if we were looking in the right direction," the sheriff said. "I guess I can let you two tag along when I go talk to Mr. Larson since you might be able to identify the suspect."

JD and I grinned.

We followed the sheriff to his patrol car where he looked up Mr. Larson's address on his computer. His eyes lit up when Larson's criminal history appeared on the screen. "Would you look at that? It seems Mr. Larson has outstanding warrants for parking tickets. Let's go pay him a visit."

We followed the sheriff to the *Largo Vista Estates* apartment complex. Deputy Perkins followed as well. The complex was a nice place with an attached marina. There were 50 units total. The grounds were well maintained.

We approached Troy's unit, apartment #29. Deputy Perkins went around back in case Troy tried to run out the back door.

The Sheriff banged on the door. He kept his hand on the grip of his holstered pistol. "Coconut County Sheriff. Open up!"

JD and I stood ready to draw our weapons if need be.

To my surprise, Troy pulled open the door. He squinted from the light and wiped the sleep from his eyes. His hair was tousled—we had clearly rousted him out of bed. Or, at least that was the impression he wanted to give us. "What's going on, Sheriff?"

"Are you supposed to work on Dan Baker's boat today?"

"Yeah. We've got an afternoon charter. I'm glad you knocked on the door, I almost overslept. I need to start getting ready."

"You don't need to get ready. Your charter has been canceled."

His face twisted. "Why? What happened?"

"Dan Baker's been killed."

"What? How?"

"I can't talk about the specifics," the sheriff said. "But I do need to ask you a few questions."

"Sure. Anything to help."

Sheriff Daniels glanced to me. I nodded. I was pretty sure this was the guy who attacked me. The voice sounded the same, though a little softer. He was the right build.

25

"Where were you this morning?" the sheriff asked.

"I've been here, sleeping," Troy said. "We had a late one last night. A few too many tequila shots."

"You got anybody that can verify that?"

"My girlfriend."

"Where can we find her?" the sheriff asked.

"Am I a suspect?"

"These are just routine questions. I gotta ask everybody."

His suspicious eyes narrowed at the sheriff. "I'm feeling like a suspect."

"What makes you feel that way?"

"Oh, I don't know. Maybe the fact that you're at my door?" Troy called into the apartment. "Hey, babe. Can you come here and tell these gentlemen where I've been all morning?"

His girlfriend sauntered to the door wearing a T-shirt and cotton men's boxers. She had no makeup and her hair was disheveled. She wasn't much of a looker, but she was a good catch for Troy. "He's been here with me. What's this about?" Then she cautioned Troy, "Don't say anything."

"I want to talk to a lawyer," Troy said.

Those were the words that every cop hated to hear. It meant you had to stop interrogating the suspect.

"I'm going to need you to come down to the station."

"Are you arresting me? What for?"

"I've got a warrant for your arrest for outstanding parking tickets. I need you to step out of the house and put your hands against the wall."

"I'm calling a lawyer," the girlfriend said. "Troy, don't say anything to these fucking pigs."

Troy didn't put up a fight. He stepped onto the porch and Sheriff Daniels ratcheted the cuffs around his wrists in no time.

"I didn't do anything," Troy protested.

"Then you've got nothing to worry about," the sheriff said.

Wayne read Troy his rights, then radioed to Deputy Perkins that he had the suspect in custody. They put Troy into the back of a patrol car, and Perkins drove him down to the station.

"You are a bunch of fucking assholes," the girlfriend shouted from the doorway.

"I don't suppose you'd let us come in and look around?" Daniels asked.

"Get fucked!" she slammed the door.

The sheriff grinned.

"Can you get a warrant to search his place?" JD asked the sheriff.

"I'll try, but I've got nothing to go on. Unless he slips up and says something incriminating, we don't have enough probable cause. And it's not like this one is going to cooperate," he said, pointing to the apartment.

"I've got an idea," I said.

The sheriff cringed. "Do I want to know?"

"Probably not," I replied.

"Just tell me what you've got in mind, and I'll pretend I didn't hear it."

"Right now, his girlfriend is getting dressed, putting on makeup, and counting how much cash they have on hand. She's going to show up at the station and pay his outstanding fines. Since you don't have enough to charge him in the death of Dan Baker, he's gonna walk away, and that's the end of it."

"Why do I feel like you're going to suggest something illegal?" the sheriff asked.

I smiled. "I'm not going to suggest anything illegal. But I think you should park a patrol car in front of the apartment. When she leaves to bail him out, I'm sure she'll forget to signal when she turns onto the highway. I would imagine you could find probable cause to search the car and the trunk. Might find a tire iron in there, but he'd be a fool to keep a murder weapon around. Might want to have divers search the marina around Dan's boat."

"Good idea," Daniels said.

"I would imagine there would be all kinds of delays in processing someone out of your jail if the computer system went down," I suggested.

The Sheriff's eyes brightened. He seemed to like the idea. "You know, I'm not very tech savvy. When that system goes down, it can take 24 to 48 hours to process someone out of the jail."

"That might give you enough time to turn up additional evidence," I said. "While the girlfriend is gone to bail him out, there will be no one at home."

"This is where I need to stop listening," the sheriff said. He knew exactly what we were going to do.

It took an hour and a half for Troy's girlfriend to pull herself together and head to the station. Sheriff Daniels followed as she pulled out of the apartment complex. She had a broken tail light. Sheriff Daniels didn't even have to make up an excuse to pull her over.

JD and I moved around to the back patio. The sliding glass door was locked, but the nearby window was open slightly. I popped off the screen, lifted the window, and climbed in. Then I let JD in through the sliding door.

We had plenty of time to search the apartment. None of it

would be admissible in a court of law. But if we found something incriminating, maybe we could figure out a way to get the evidence legally. I needed to know beyond a shadow of a doubt if this was the man who attacked me and threatened Madison. I didn't want to take justice into my own hands, but I would if necessary.

26

I figured we had at least several hours to search this place. Probably more. Troy's girlfriend wasn't going to get through the maze of paperwork anytime soon.

We searched high and low, turning the place upside down. We put everything back as we found it. I looked in all the places you would normally hide things—under mattresses, in air ducts, under furniture. I even looked for hidden floorboards and removable baseboards.

The murder weapon didn't turn up.

But we did find something of interest.

Troy had a freezer full of fish. They were wrapped in white butcher paper, and clearly labeled—Marlin, Swordfish, Tuna, Mahi-Mahi. Nothing unusual for someone who worked on a charter fishing boat. I grabbed one of the packages. It didn't feel like frozen fish.

It felt like a brick.

I unwrapped the butcher paper and found a kilo of cocaine.

JD's eyes widened. "It's party time."

If everything labeled fish in the freezer was cocaine, there were at least 50 kilos.

"At least we know what he's into," I said.

"I'd say that's about $4 million worth of cocaine wholesale in Miami," JD said.

"That's a lot of product," I said. "Where would the front money come from?"

JD shrugged. "Maybe Dan was in on it. He fronted the money. Troy gets greedy. Who knows?"

I shook my head. "Dan didn't have that kind of money. He just got divorced. He said everything he had was tied up in the boat. I think they got fronted this on consignment."

"That's a lot of product to sell on consignment," JD said.

I shook my head. "Not really. If they moved a few small loads successfully, built up a little credibility, it's not a stretch at all. Everybody knows what happens when you screw over the Colombians, so people don't often steal from them."

A devious idea popped into my head.

"Oh no," JD said. "I know that look."

"It would be a shame for all this cocaine to go missing. Troy would have to answer a lot of questions. He'd have to deal with some really angry people."

I grabbed a rolling suitcase from the hall closet and loaded it full of the packages of *fish*. I left a few kilos behind just to rub it in. And more than enough for him to go away for a long time if Sheriff Daniels got a warrant.

JD hid a few of his small wireless cameras around the apartment. They were smaller than a shirt button. With an adhesive back, he stuck one on the frame of the TV by the logo, another on the coffee maker in the kitchen, and one on the TV in the bedroom. They provided a high-definition, wide-angle view, with audio.

JD was able to access the feed from his cell phone. We could watch the surveillance footage from anywhere with an Internet connection.

None of that would be usable in court, but when Troy got back home and realized how much trouble he was in, there were going to be more than a few heated conversations about it. And hopefully, we'd learned the details about his operation.

With any luck, maybe the Colombians would take care of my problem for me?

I rolled the suitcase full of cocaine behind me and stepped onto the patio. JD locked the door from the inside, then climbed out the open window and replaced the screen. Each patio was separated by a fence, but there was an open view of the marina through a wrought-iron gate.

"What exactly do you plan on doing with that?" JD asked, eyeing the suitcase.

"I've got a place in mind for it."

"You realize that stuff is illegal, and if we get caught with it, we're going down for a long time."

I shrugged. "We better not get caught."

JD tensed. "If we do, there goes my car, my boat, my house."

I thought about it for a moment. I knelt down and pried a heavy stone from the ground that rimmed the flower bed. I shoved it into the suitcase to weight it down, then strolled through the gate, onto the dock. The wheels of the case rattled against the wood plank as I pulled it to the end of the marina. I swung the roll-case into the air, and it splashed into the water. The case floated for a few moments, then filled with water and sunk to the bottom of the channel.

"$4 million," JD muttered.

"Troy is in a whole lot of trouble." I smiled.

We made our way back to the parking lot, and JD drove me back to the marina at *Diver Down*. He had to run a few errands and took off.

I stepped inside the bar to check on Alejandro. Things were running smoothly. I grabbed a bite to eat, then strolled down the dock to the *Slick'n Salty*. I was quite surprised at what I found.

27

"**I** thought you had a flight to catch," I said, pleasantly surprised.

Aria sat in the cockpit with a beaming smile. She shrugged. "I told my friends to go back without me. I'll catch up in a few days. I hope you don't mind."

I smiled, glad to see her. "No. I don't mind at all."

"It's almost happy hour. What do you say we grab a drink, maybe some dinner? Who knows, if you play your cards right, you might get lucky."

That sounded damn fine to me. "I've got to warn you though, I'm pretty good at cards."

"I know." Her sultry eyes sparkled.

We caught a cab over to Oyster Avenue. It was a popular tourist destination, lined with bars and restaurants. Live music, overpriced drinks, and large crowds. There was everything from the casual dive bar to the upscale swanky eatery. You could catch a local blues band at *Jimmy Ray's*, or dance to techno music at *Starfish*.

We grabbed a few drinks at *Reefers*—reggae music and Caribbean cuisine. All the waitresses wore skimpy bikini tops and jean shorts. It was a common theme on the island. We sat at a cocktail table close to the bar.

A familiar voice tickled my ear. "Funny seeing you here, stranger."

I was surprised to see Scarlett's smiling face. "I didn't know you worked here."

"I pick up a few shifts here and there. It's just temporary."

I introduced Jack's daughter to Aria.

"Oh my God, you're Aria," Scarlett said, star-struck. "Like, THE Aria!"

Aria smiled shyly.

"I've been following you for years. Your lifestyle seems so glamorous."

"I can't lie. It is a lot of fun."

Scarlett surveyed the two of us. "So, are you two like a *thing*?"

She enjoyed putting us on the spot.

I fumbled for words, then decided it was best to let Aria answer that question.

"Um, we are seeing where this thing goes," Aria said with a lustful glimmer in her eyes.

"Well, he's definitely a keeper," Scarlett added.

Aria and I both knew this was probably just a vacation romance. She was going back to New York in the near future. Neither one of us had any illusions about the reality of it and how ill-fated it probably was. But we were both enjoying ourselves.

"Can I start you off with anything? Cocktails, appetizers?"

"Cocktails for sure," Aria said.

"The daiquiris are really great here. Not that I would know," she added, having clearly indulged in them.

"Two strawberry daiquiris it is," Aria said.

Usually I stayed away from the fruity drinks and stuck with the professional stuff—whiskey, vodka, aged rum—but a daiquiri sounded pretty tasty, and I didn't want to disappoint the lady.

"Coming right up," Scarlett said. She spun around and sauntered toward the bar.

"That's Jack's daughter?" Aria asked, stunned.

"I know, right?"

"She's gorgeous. She's wasting her talent here. She could make a killing modeling."

"Maybe you can give her some pointers?" I said.

Aria smiled. "I'd be happy to."

Scarlett returned a few moments later with strawberry daiquiris so cold they'd give you an ice headache if you drank them too fast. "Are you ready to order, or do you need a few minutes?"

"Give us a few minutes," I said.

"Just holler when you need me." She trotted away, attending to the next table—a bunch of drunk bikers. They were loud, obnoxious, inappropriate, and a little handsy. Scarlett kept her distance from the table, and I could tell she didn't like serving them.

When Scarlett returned to take our order, I asked, "Are those guys giving you any trouble?"

She glanced over to the bikers. "Who? Those guys? Nothing I can't handle. This place is usually cool, but now and then the creepers come in."

They saw us looking and clearly knew we were discussing them. A burly redheaded guy with a beard wearing a denim biker jacket scowled at me, as if I was supposed to be afraid.

I wasn't looking for trouble and just wanted to have a nice afternoon, so I ignored them.

"We're going to have to do a complete evaluation of your social media presence," Aria said to Scarlett. "You're going to become my pet project. Do what I say, and you'll have a million followers within the next six months."

Scarlett's eyes brightened, filled with dreams of Internet stardom. "Oh, my God, thank you! That would be so amazing. You really think that I can do what you do?"

"Absolutely, girl. You got it going on."

"Okay. This is so awesome. I'll be back." Scarlett flitted away on cloud nine.

"You gotta stick to your word. You can't get her hopes up like that and not follow through."

Aria feigned offense. "Do I look like someone who wouldn't follow through? I meant what I said. I'll help her out. Once she gets her profile ready, all I have to do is shout out to my followers about my hot new friend, and boom, overnight sensation."

I took an uncertain breath. "JD is going to kill me."

"Why?"

"He can barely keep her in line as it is. What do you think's going to happen when she's InstaFamous?"

"Give her a little credit. She'll keep it together. I'll give her tips on more than just social media. We'll talk about finances, investments, Roth IRAs."

I raised an impressed eyebrow.

Off my surprised reaction, she said, "What? Do you think I'm blowing through my cash like a fool? I'm well aware that these looks and this body aren't going to last forever. I plan to have enough cash socked away to retire by 30 and keep living the lifestyle I'm accustomed to. If I can parlay my celebrity into something after that, great. If not, I'll continue to travel, maybe write a book, who knows? Perhaps I'll fall in love and start a family?"

She batted her eyelashes at me.

"Glad to see you have a plan."

"I'm not as shallow and as ditzy as you thought, am I?"

"I never thought that," I said, putting on my best poker face.

She coughed the word, "Liar."

We downed a few daiquiris, talked, laughed, and enjoyed

each other's company. For a moment, I forgot all about my troubles. I ordered the jerked chicken, and she got the soft-shell crab.

Then my phone rang.

Unknown caller.

I knew exactly who it was. I didn't want to answer. "Will you excuse me while I take this?"

"Sure, go ahead."

I cringed as I answered the phone. "Isabella. So nice to hear from you."

I smiled through gritted teeth.

28

Aria's eyes narrowed at me. I could see the flame of jealousy burning in them.

"Are you staying out of trouble, Tyson?" Isabella asked.

"Sort of. What do you want?"

"I thought you'd like to know that we still haven't found Cartwright. Though he did take a significant cash payout from a rival cartel to put the hit on Ruiz."

"Told you."

"It looks like you're off the hook. Say *thank you*."

"Thank you."

"As such, you're back on active status. It took a lot of convincing on my part, but I assured everyone that you are still reliable and at the top of your game."

"That is extremely kind of you, Isabella," I said dryly. "But I'm retiring."

"Excuse me?"

"You heard me. I'm done. I'm out."

There was a long silence.

"Tyson, there is no *out*."

"Yes, there is."

"You know old spies don't retire. They die."

"Who are you calling old?"

"Exactly. You've got plenty of ops left in you."

"I'm done. I'm telling you."

"We'll see about that. I can be very persuasive." Isabella hung up the phone. Her version of gentle persuasion was putting a gun to your head. Sometimes literally, sometimes figuratively. I didn't like the sound of that.

"Girlfriend?" Aria asked, trying to conceal her jealousy. "I mean, it's cool if you've got a girlfriend. I know we're just…"

"Not my girlfriend."

"Ex?" she asked. "Sorry, it's none of my business."

"Not my ex. Former business associate. She doesn't want me to leave the company. But I've decided to make a life change."

"Working for JD?"

"Something like that."

Aria smiled, relieved. We liked each other more than either one of us were letting on.

Scarlett brought us another round of daiquiris just as our current drinks bottomed out, and the last bit of the sweet liquid rattled through our straws.

Scarlett checked on the neighboring table of bikers who had grown even more rowdy. Their comments grew more vulgar. One of them grabbed Scarlett and pulled her a little too close for comfort. His hand found its way from the small of her back to her ass, grabbing an unwelcome handful.

She extricated herself from the situation and gave him an earful before storming off to tell her manager she refused to wait on them anymore.

By that time, I had put my napkin down. "Excuse me for a moment. I need to take care of this."

"What are you going to do?"

Aria watched with concerned eyes. To the average person, it looked like a suicide mission. There were four bikers at the table—all barrel chested men with thick forearms and tattoos. Some of them prison tats. These weren't your weekend warrior Wall Street guys who had plunked down $25,000 for a Harley. These were criminals. No doubt about it.

"I think it's time for you boys to pay your tab and leave," I said. "And apologize to the lady."

The table laughed.

"Who's going to make us? You?" the red-haired man said. He was clearly the leader of the gang and spoke for his companions.

"It's going to be real embarrassing when I kick your ass," I said.

Red laughed again. "You got balls. I'll give you that."

"So I've been told."

Chairs screeched against the concrete as the four of them pushed away from the table and stood up. These guys towered over me.

"Last chance," I warned.

"You sure are a mouthy little fart."

"Do you boys have health insurance? I mean, I'll try to go easy on you, but ER visits are expensive. And I'm pretty sure all of you will need to be admitted for serious injuries."

"Can you believe this guy?" Red said, chuckling. "You know, I almost like you. I mean, hell, anybody willing to stand up to us deserves a little respect. Why don't you join us for a beer?"

"Sorry. I don't drink with scumbags."

I guess Red had enough of my smart mouth because he took a swing.

I ducked, jabbed a fist in his belly, then spun around and put an elbow into his nose. Blood spewed, and bones crumpled. He fell back and crashed against the cocktail table. Drinks scattered, and bottles smashed against the floor. Amber shards of glass danced, and beer foamed.

His companions looked stunned.

One of them charged toward me. He swung a hard right.

I blocked his forearm, slammed my fist into his rib cage, then finished with a knee to the groin and an elbow to the back of the neck.

Another goon attacked. He jabbed twice, then swung a left hook.

I bobbed and weaved.

His wide swing left him vulnerable, and I clocked him in the jaw, then jammed my foot into the side of his knee. His ligaments snapped, and the ogre dropped to the ground, screaming in agony.

The last goon raised his hands in surrender, backing away. He scampered out of the bar, leaving his friends to fend for themselves.

Bar patrons cheered.

Scarlett watched, both stunned and elated.

"Call the cops," I said. "And you better call an ambulance."

Scarlett ran to me and gave me a hug. "Thank you. Those guys were jerks. You could have gotten hurt!"

"Nonsense. I just needed to teach them a lesson in respect," I said.

I went back to my table to finish the meal.

Aria was impressed—and a little bit turned on. "What was your old job? UFC fighter?"

I laughed. "No. Way more dangerous."

Her eyes sparkled. "I have to say, you are probably the most interesting man I've ever dated."

"So, we're dating?" I asked, playfully.

"It sounds better than *hooking up*, doesn't it?" She smiled. "And speaking of hooking up... There's nothing more romantic than fighting for a woman's honor. What do you say we find someplace a little more private, and you can show me what other moves you've got?"

"That sounds reasonable to me."

"Unless you like the public thing? I'm sure we could find someplace dangerous." She had a deliciously naughty glimmer in her eyes.

———

29

The manager comped our meal, and I left Scarlett a healthy tip.

Sheriff Daniels showed up and took one look at me and shook his head. "Do you just go out looking for trouble?"

"It has a way of finding me."

"Want to tell me what happened?"

I gave him the short version of the story.

"By the way, the divers found a crowbar in the channel near the *Heartbreaker*. The ME says it could be the murder weapon, but it's likely no trace evidence will be recovered. We probably won't be able to tie it to Troy."

"Do you still have him locked up?"

The sheriff smiled. "Those darn computers. He won't be out before morning."

I grinned.

Daniels and Deputy Perkins arrested the bikers after the EMTs treated their wounds.

"So, you're helping the police with a murder investigation?" Aria asked.

"I'm... consulting here and there."

Her eyes sparkled again. "Just when I thought you couldn't get any more interesting..."

I knew a great spot to catch the sunset that might fulfill Aria's experimental desires. I said goodbye to Scarlett, and we left *Reefers*. We strolled down Oyster Avenue, heading toward the beach.

Tours of the Coconut Key lighthouse ended at 4:30 PM. No one lived on the property, and it was easy to pick the lock to the lighthouse itself. It was a cast-iron tower built in the 1840s. It had undergone several renovations over the years and now was a museum and gift shop.

I can neither confirm, nor deny, what happened on the steps inside the tower, or the catwalk around the giant Fresnel light that once warned sailors of the rocky shore. But if something naughty did occur, it was a lot of fun.

Afterward, we watched the sun disappear over the horizon from the top of the tower. The ocean breeze blew our hair, and the last rays of amber light bounced off our retinas. The sky was alive with glorious shades of pink, purple, blue, and orange. Aria wrapped her arms around me with her head against my chest. It was a nice, quiet moment.

JD called. "I heard you went medieval on some jackasses at *Reefers*."

"Just had to put some people in their place."

"Scarlett told me all about it. Thanks for looking out for her. I owe you one."

"You don't owe me anything."

"I've always got your back. You know that."

"I know."

"Scarlett tells me you were with that little honey from the boat. I thought she skipped town?"

"She delayed her return trip. What can I say, I have a magnetic personality," I said with a smile.

Aria knew I was talking about her.

"Careful now," JD said. "She might be habit-forming."

"That she is."

Aria and I snuck out of the lighthouse and made our way back to Oyster Avenue. We hit a few bars, then called it an early night and took an Uber back to the boat. We tumbled around the sheets, making waves, doing our best to wear each other out. She was insatiable, and I felt like I was back in college again.

The sheriff called the next day to give me a heads up that he was about to release Troy Larson. "Just thought you might want to know. We couldn't pull any evidence that connects Troy to the tire iron. Hell, we don't even know if it was the same tire iron used to kill Dan Baker. The water degraded any evidence that may have existed. The DA doesn't think we have enough to get an indictment. And the judge won't issue a search warrant. Looks like the guy's going to walk."

"He's not going to walk," I assured him. "I can't tell you how it got there, but in the marina behind Troy Larson's apartment, you'll find a rolling suitcase with his name on it. Inside is $4 million worth of cocaine."

"I'm not even going to ask. I'll have some divers pull it out of the water. But that's not going to stick. He's going to say the suitcase was stolen."

"I don't care if it sticks or not. He's got a lot of explaining to do to his supplier. The fireworks should be starting soon. I'll touch base shortly."

"I don't know what kind of crazy scheme you and JD cooked up, but watch your back. You might be getting in over your head."

"I'm used to that kind of thing."

"I don't doubt it."

It was a few hours later when I got a call from JD. "I'm on my way over. It's showtime."

JD was at the boat within minutes, and we watched a live feed on his cell phone from the cameras we had placed in Troy's apartment.

Troy had returned and discovered his merchandise was missing. He flew into a rampage, cussing and screaming and breaking things.

Troy looked like a wild animal, punching holes in the sheet rock, turning over furniture, rummaging through the apartment.

"I'm telling you, it was those goddamn cops," his girlfriend shouted.

"Cops don't break into your apartment and steal your stash," Troy said.

"Dirty ones do. You know that fat fuck is on the take."

"No. It's Garrett. That bastard is trying to double-cross me. He's the only one that knew it was here."

"What about Luke?" she asked.

"No. He just got out of jail."

"What are you going to do?"

It seemed that all three of them were in on it. I was starting to get a better picture of their operation.

Troy snatched his cell phone from his pocket and called Garrett. He tried to play it cool and not sound upset. Troy told Garrett he needed to see him ASAP.

Aria watched the video with wide eyes. "Is this for real?"

"Afraid so," JD said.

"This is better than reality TV."

There was a half-hour of bickering between Troy and his girlfriend, then Garrett arrived. As soon as he stepped into the apartment, Troy put a gun to his head. "Where is it?"

"Where is what, man?" Garrett's face twisted with confusion.

30

G arrett was tall, well-built, with short red hair and freckles. He wore a trimmed beard and was probably about 6'2".

Troy was practically frothing at the mouth. His finger was wrapped tight around the trigger of his 9mm.

It was a precarious situation.

The slightest twitch, and the weapon would go off. To say that Troy was unstable would be an understatement.

"Where is it?" Troy asked.

"What are you talking about?" Garrett replied.

"The coke, you piece of shit," Troy's girlfriend shouted. "It's gone! What did you do with it?"

"I didn't do anything with it. You told me it was in your freezer."

"It was," Troy said.

"Wait! Are you saying it's gone?" Garrett asked.

"Don't play stupid with me," Troy shouted.

"You don't really think I took it?"

"I want answers. Now. I swear to God, I'll blow your head off!" Troy shoved the shaky gun in Garrett's face.

"Look, man. Just calm down."

"Don't tell me to calm down!" Troy shouted. "I'm going to count to three, and if you don't tell me where it is, I'm pulling the trigger."

Garrett's eyes welled as he pleaded for his life. "I didn't take it, man."

"1..."

"Come on, bro!"

"2..."

"Dude, please!" Tears streamed down Garrett's cheeks. He was about to have a nervous breakdown, and Troy was about to go mental.

"3..."

A knock on the door was the only thing that saved Garrett.

Troy grimaced and paused for a moment.

"I didn't take the stuff, I swear," Garrett whispered.

Another series of knocks interrupted the tense moment.

"Go see who it is," Troy commanded.

Troy's girlfriend scampered down the foyer to the door. "What do you want?"

A man's muffled voice filtered through the door. "Can you keep it down? I gotta work the graveyard shift."

The girlfriend was offscreen. I couldn't see her, but it sounded like she pulled open the door. She talked with a neighbor for a moment, then she moved back into the living room. "Carl said he saw two guys on the patio, leaving with a suitcase."

Troy took a moment to process the information, then pulled the gun away from Garrett's head. "When?"

"Yesterday. Shortly after you were arrested. Said one guy looked like a rock star from the 80s. It was those two guys that were with the sheriff."

"They broke into the house and stole my stash?" Troy said, coming to the realization.

"It sure as hell wasn't me," Garrett said.

Troy's whole body tensed. "We're all dead if we don't find that stash, or come up with the money."

"This is all because you killed Jeremy," Garrett said.

Troy snarled at him. "I had to."

"You brought the heat down on all of us," Garrett said. "I can't believe you thought I'd fuck you over. We've been best friends since grade school."

"Just shut up. I'm the only one who had the balls to do what needed to be done. Jeremy stole from us, and I had to lay down the law. You cannot show weakness in this business."

"Jeremy didn't steal from us, man. He got ripped off."

"Either way. Not my problem," Troy said. "Just like it's not going to be Enrique's problem that we don't have his cash. The Colombians are going to take us all out, and everyone we know. We've got to get that coke back."

"How are we going to do that?"

The video feed dropped out. The screen filled with digital static.

"What's going on?" I asked.

JD shrugged. "Shitty Internet? I don't know."

"So, let me get this straight... Did you guys steal some dude's cocaine?" Aria asked.

"No," I said, innocently. "We just put it somewhere he'll never find it."

"Why would you do that?"

"Remember that murder investigation that I'm helping the police with?"

"Yeah?" she said, having second thoughts about our relationship.

"Well, it has to do with that. It's complicated."

"You are quickly going from *interesting* to *psychotic*. You realize that, don't you?"

"Don't rush to judgment," I said.

Her blue eyes narrowed at me. "Those guys looked pretty pissed off. It sounds like they're coming for you."

"Yeah. Pretty much."

"Doesn't that bother you?"

"Nothing I can't handle," I said, casually.

Aria shrugged. "You seemed to handle yourself pretty well at *Reefers*."

"Trust me," JD said. "The man can take care of himself."

"Things might get a little crazy around here. It might be safer for you if you went back to your hotel. Better yet, back to New York. Not that I want you to go."

"If you are as good as you say you are, then I've got nothing to worry about," Aria said with a smile.

"I like her," JD said. "She's got spunk."

"Thank you, JD," she said.

"Just do me a favor and go back to the hotel until we get this sorted," I pleaded.

"You're not trying to run me out to make room for another little hottie, are you?" She was half joking.

"No. No other hotties."

"Good." Her perfect teeth sparkled as she smiled again.

"You know, Scarlett's not safe either," I said. "They're going to come for both of us. You know that?"

"You're right. I'll take this one home," JD said pointing to Aria. "Then I'll send Scarlett up to my mom's place in Miami until this blows over. She's not going to be happy about leaving."

I escorted Aria down the dock and saw her off. She climbed into Jack's Porsche and waved as the car sped out of the parking lot.

I went back to the boat, grabbed a pair of night vision goggles, and climbed up to the bridge. I sat there with my 9mm, waiting.

31

T roy wasn't going to waste any time. He needed his cocaine back. He was going to come for me, or JD, tonight.

I'm sure in their minds, they thought they'd be able to capture me and beat me until I told them where the coke was. But these guys were amateurs.

Still, I wanted to make sure they weren't able to gain any leverage. With Madison in South Beach, Scarlett on her way to Miami, and Aria safe in her hotel, I could focus on one thing—bringing these assholes down.

I figured all I needed to do was sit back and let them come to me.

It had taken some doing, but JD finally convinced Scarlett to get on the road. She didn't want to leave her friends and apparently had a date that she would have to break. Somehow JD convinced her it was in her best interest to leave. He didn't say how much cash he had to give her as a bribe, but I got the impression it was quite a lot.

Jack returned to the marina with a Köenig-Haas SA-25 semi-automatic, special applications sniper rifle. It was chambered in 7.62mm. It shared over 60% of its parts with the AR-15, making it highly customizable. It had a 20-inch barrel, high-capacity magazine, key-mod rail system, and a suppressor (which Jack had an NFA tax stamp for, so it was completely legal). The weapon had been adopted by SOCOM and was also used by IDF forces.

Needless to say, it was a capable weapon.

We planned on using a standard tactic—make yourself an easy target and draw enemy fire. Then ambush as they closed in.

We decided it was best for Jack to take an Overwatch position in Madison's loft above the bar. Through an open window, he would have excellent coverage of the parking lot, dock, and the *Slick'n Salty*.

I turned the lights in the deckhouse on and made sure the stereo was up loud enough to filter across the water, hoping to draw the thugs out. I bunched the pillows up in the bed to make it look like someone was sleeping in the master state-room. Then I positioned myself on a neighboring boat and waited for the assault. Ernie was out of town, and I didn't think he'd mind.

Jack and I communicated with each other via wireless earbuds. It was like the old Special Ops days. The rush of adrenaline coursed through my veins, and it made me miss being on the job.

I figured Troy would strike between 3 and 4 AM. That gave us quite a bit of *hurry up and wait* time.

JD's voice crackled in my earbud. "That girl likes you."

"You think?"

"It's pretty obvious. She couldn't stop talking about you on the way back to the hotel."

"She'll forget all about me the minute she gets back to New York."

"I wouldn't be so sure about that."

"It's Coconut Key," I said. "You can't take anything seriously down here. Tourists come and go. Always have, always will."

"You don't have to play it cool for me. Go on, admit it. You kind of like her."

"Alright. I'll admit it. Spending time with her hasn't exactly been painful."

"Just don't get too involved with this girl and forget about your friends."

"Stop. Just stop right now." He was going to harass me all night long. I could tell.

We sat there and waited, and waited, and waited...

3 AM came and went.

Then 4 AM...

Then my phone buzzed. *Unknown caller.*

I didn't have time for Isabella now. I ignored the call and sent it to voicemail.

Whoever it was didn't leave a message.

A moment later, my phone buzzed again. This time I decided I'd better answer it.

"If you want to see the girl alive again, you'll bring me my stuff."

My body tensed, and my stomach twisted in knots. This was a call I never wanted to receive. I put it on speakerphone so it would filter through the comm link to JD.

"You want me to bring your stuff and you'll let the girl go?" I asked. It was an FBI mirroring tactic. Repeating keywords would spur the kidnapper to repeat his demands and perhaps reveal additional information.

"Yes. That's what I said. Are you deaf?"

"I just want to make sure I'm hearing you correctly so that I can comply with your demands."

"Bring me the 50 kilos of cocaine, and I will let the girl go. Do you need me to speak slower?"

"Put her on the phone," I said. "I want proof of life."

"No," Troy barked. "You bring what you stole from me."

"I need proof of life, otherwise there is no incentive for me to comply. This is a two-way street."

It was only a few seconds before I heard her voice, but it seemed like an eternity. During that unbearable moment, my mind raced, not knowing who they had taken. I was crushed when I finally heard her voice. It wasn't real until then, like Schrödinger's cat existing in a state of infinite possibilities. *Infinitely bad possibilities.*

32

"Tyson?" a frail, trembling voice said. That one word conveyed a host of emotions.

"Have they hurt you?" I asked.

Before Scarlett answered, Troy yanked the phone away. "Happy? She's alive. If you want her to stay that way you've got two hours to return my merchandise."

"You want me to return the merchandise within two hours?"

"Yes. The longer you drag this out, the more inclined I am to cause irreparable harm to this young lady."

"I need a little time to get it."

"You don't have my merchandise?"

"Relax. I put it someplace safe."

Troy growled. "You better bring it back to me. All of it. If so much as an ounce is missing, she dies."

"I've got it. Every last ounce." I paused. "You're not having a good day, are you?"

"No. I'm not. Thanks to assholes like you."

"Sorry about that. I bet you boys will be in a lot of trouble if you don't get that merchandise?"

"You're goddamn right!"

"You've got every right to be angry," I said.

I was trying to get him talking and build rapport. I didn't know if it was working.

"Take your boat out of the harbor and head south. I'm going to text you coordinates. You'll wait there for further instructions." He paused. "You seem like a smart guy. So I'm sure I don't need to tell you... No cops. No feds. Just you and that washed up '80s wanna-be friend of yours. Unarmed. Are we clear?"

"Clear."

Troy hung up.

"Did you get all that?" I said to JD.

"Yeah, I got it" he said, stunned.

"Don't worry. We're going to get her back."

"I watched Scarlett get in the car and drive away," JD muttered in disbelief, still trying to process how this happened. "When we get her back, I'm going to strangle her. She doesn't listen to a thing I say! I'm going to call her friend, Ella, and see if she knows anything. I'll meet you at the boat."

When Jack boarded the *Slick'n Salty,* he paced the deck nervously. The wheels turned behind his eyes, calculating scenarios and possibilities. He held together pretty well, despite the situation. He compartmentalized and pushed it into that part of his brain where it was just another op.

I could see in his face that if he let the full magnitude of the situation sink in, he'd break down and lose it. But Jack wouldn't allow himself to go there. Not when we had a job to do.

"Ella said Scarlett had a date with some guy. Aiden. Ella didn't have his number. I bet Scarlett turned around and went straight to meet him," JD said. "Troy and his bunch were probably watching my house and followed her."

"I'm sorry, Jack. This is my fault. I should never have taken his stash. It blew up in our faces."

Jack frowned. "Not your fault. Well, maybe just a little."

A regretful frown tugged at my lips.

"We'll take the boat over to the marina, dive down, grab the coke, and make the swap," Jack said.

I cringed. "Slight problem. I told the sheriff where to find it. It's probably sitting in an evidence locker right now."

"So, we call the sheriff and get him to loan us the evidence, and he can get it back when we make the trade." Jack was understandably a little frazzled. His wide eyes and trembling hands gave him away.

"Jack, you're not thinking clearly. The sheriff is not going to give us $4 million worth of cocaine."

"It never hurts to ask," JD said. He pulled his phone from his pocket.

"What are you doing?"

"Calling Wayne."

"Even if he does give us the stash, those guys have no intention of letting us all walk away. Two people are already dead."

Wayne's groggy voice filtered through the phone. "Sheriff Daniels."

"Sheriff, Jack Donovan."

"Jack, it's 4:30 AM. This better be good."

"About that cocaine you recovered from the marina..."

Wayne paused. "We didn't recover any cocaine."

"You didn't?" Jack said, perplexed.

I could hear the sheriff's thin voice. My eyes widened with surprise.

"I sent divers down," Wayne said. "They couldn't find anything. Can we talk about this at a more reasonable hour?"

"Sure, no problem," JD stammered. He disconnected the call. "Looks like somebody else found it first."

I deflated, kicking myself for taking it in the first place. "Great. Somebody's running around with 50 kilos."

"Now what?"

"It's your call. We can call the feds and let them handle it, or we do it our way."

"This wouldn't be the first time we've negotiated for a hostage," Jack said. "And I don't want anybody else screwing it up. We recovered those journalists back in Iraq. We rescued the ambassador in Afghanistan. This is no different."

"These guys are backed into a corner. They're inexperienced, and they're panicking. They'll be prone to making stupid decisions, which is good and bad. They know that if they don't come up with that cocaine, or the money, they're dead. They've got nothing to lose, and that makes them dangerous."

"Well, they pissed me off, and that makes me way more dangerous."

"We'll get her back, Jack," I assured.

I slipped my phone from my pocket and made a call that I hoped I would never have to make.

"Who are you calling?" JD asked.

"Just getting us a little tactical assistance."

33

A sleepy female voice filtered from my phone. "What do you want?"

"I'm shocked," I said. "I didn't think you ever slept. I thought you were a cold, ruthless machine."

"I am a machine," Isabella said. "Is this a booty call, or is this business?"

"I need your help."

"*Quid pro quo*, Tyson."

My agreement to her terms was implicit in our continuing the conversation. It meant that somewhere down the line, she was going to call me and make a request—and I would have to do the job, no matter what it was. "I need you to find someone for me."

"I thought you were retired?"

"This is a personal matter."

"You should know better than to get involved in personal matters."

"Circumstances beyond my control."

"Since I won't be able to get back to sleep, who am I trying to find?" Isabella asked.

"I received a call on this phone a few minutes ago. I need the location of the caller."

"I'll see what I can do." Isabella hung up.

"Did you just make a deal with the devil?" JD asked.

"I think so."

Madison had left me her keys to *Diver Down*. JD and I fumbled through the kitchen and found flour, Ziploc bags, and butcher paper. We made 50 fake kilos, wrapped them in duct tape, then covered them with butcher paper. We labeled them as various fillets of fish and stuffed them into a rolling suitcase that I took from Madison's loft. The subterfuge wouldn't last long, but maybe it would buy us a few minutes. In these types of situations, every second counts.

By the time we were done with our craft project, Isabella texted me the coordinates of their location. I showed my phone screen to JD.

"That looks like half-a-mile south of Urchin Key," he said.

"I know it. Small little strip of an island about 2 miles offshore."

We pulled the area up on the maps app.

"If we take this route," I said, pointing to the screen, "you can drop me off here. I can take the tender to the north side of the island. From there, I should be able to get a view of their boat with night vision. I can slip into the water on the south side with the Dräger and come up underneath their boat. You can rendezvous with them as scheduled. Before they realize I'm not with you, I'll be on their boat and will have neutralized the threat."

"I like the way that sounds. Let's hope it goes as smoothly as you make it sound."

"It will."

"Be careful in that water, that area is full of bull sharks. And they are aggressive."

"If I don't bother them, they won't bother me," I said, hopeful.

We boarded Jack's boat and pulled the tender from storage. It was a 7.5-foot inflatable *WavePro MK-II*. The pontoons were gray and black, and it had a *Barracuda MM7* electric motor that would run the tender at close to 6 knots. The motor was whisper quiet, and if the wind was right, they'd never hear me coming. If I needed absolute silence, there were two 6-inch aluminum ores. But rowing against the wind in a dinghy wasn't my idea of fun.

I don't know how Jack got his hands on it, but he had a military issue Dräger LAR V closed-circuit oxygen rebreather. It was the preferred diving apparatus for stealth units. Low noise, no bubbles, compact and streamlined.

We cast off, left the marina, and headed south. JD throttled up and brought the boat on plane.

A storm brewed offshore.

The occasional flash of lightning and ripple of thunder rolled across the sky. The conditions were okay, but deteriorating rapidly. The front rolled in from the southeast, and the winds picked up.

A text from Troy came through with the rendezvous coordinates. They were about 2 miles south of the location Isabella had given me.

My hunch was that Troy intended to send us to a temporary location and let us sit for a while to make sure we were alone. Then they'd give us coordinates to their actual location. If they were smart, they'd have a spotter near the fake rendezvous point, looking for law enforcement.

Jack cut the engines about a mile north of Urchin Key. The rain was coming down in sheets now.

We tossed the tender into the water and I loaded it with my gear, which included nightvision goggles, Jack's sniper rifle, the Dräger, fins, and a K-Bar knife.

I climbed over the transom and stepped into the tender. The waves rocked the tiny boat. I looked up at JD, his eyes full of concern.

"We got this," I said. "No worries."

34

The little electric motor was good for six hours at full throttle. The wind was out of the southeast. With the storm, there was no way the sound of the little motor would carry across the island.

Wind rushed through my hair. Hard rain and the spray of salt water pelted my face. The soft bottom of the tender didn't allow it to get on plane, but I was moving at a decent speed, probably cruising along at 4 knots. The rolling waves felt like a roller coaster as the tiny craft pitched up and down. I hit the north side of the island in 15 minutes. I hopped out of the craft and pulled the tender up the beach to the tree line.

I put on my tactical helmet and pulled down my night vision goggles (NVGs). My surroundings lit up with a green glow as I looked through the optics. I shouldered the Dräger, grabbed my fins and sniper rifle, and headed south across the island, weaving through mangrove trees and underbrush.

At the south shore, I posted up behind a tree and scanned the horizon. The *Heartbreaker* was just where Isabella said it was. Maybe half a mile from shore.

I strapped on the Dräger and donned my mask. The unit hung from my chest, unlike a traditional scuba tank. It was good for about four hours of use. I slipped into the water, put on my fins, and submerged.

A solo dive at night is extremely dangerous. Especially a covert one. There's no one to save you if you get in trouble. Boats can't see you when you're wearing a black suit and gear. It's difficult to see and easy to get disoriented. But this wasn't my first rodeo.

A night dive in a busy harbor in freezing cold water to place a limpet mine on a ship's hull can be much more dangerous than diving the Keys.

Twenty minutes later, I could see the hull of the target vessel. I ascended to the stern of the boat and hovered just under the surface, listening. I could hear muffled voices reverberating through the hull.

The water was only 20 feet deep here. I ditched the Dräger, mask, and fins, letting them sink to the bottom. If all went well, I could retrieve my gear later.

I hovered by the swim platform as the waves crashed against the fiberglass hull. The boat pitched and rolled in the turbulent seas.

"Would you just calm down," Troy muttered. "This is the only way."

"I don't know, man," Garrett said, panicked. "This has gotten out of hand."

"Once we get the stuff, we kill them and the girl," Troy said. "If we don't, they're going to go straight to the cops, and we'll all go down. Is that what you want?"

"No."

"Then man-up."

Troy's girlfriend's voice crackled through a walkie-talkie, "I see them. They're at the first rendezvous point."

"Are they alone?" Troy asked.

"Yeah. I think so."

"Give it a few minutes, then report back," Troy said.

"I don't know, man. How is this going to work out?" Garrett asked.

"Don't worry," Troy said. "Luke is going to take care of it."

I heard another person enter the cockpit and set down dive tanks. They clanked against the deck. It must have been Luke, Dan's first mate. They were all in this together.

"I've got a Russian SK-7 limpet mine. When they come to make the exchange, I'll swim over and attach the mine to their engine. They won't make it back to port. That's for certain."

"Where the hell did you get that?" Garrett asked.

"Same place I got the guns and the C4."

Luke sat on the gunwale and prepped his dive gear. I hovered by the stern with my head just barely out of the water, waiting to make my move.

After a few minutes, Troy's girlfriend's voice crackled back through the walkie, "I think they're alone. There's nobody else out here."

"Give it one last look with the night vision," Troy said.

"I'm telling you, there's no one else out here. It's not like they've got a team of Navy SEALs hiding under the water. I'm coming back. I have been sitting out here for an hour in this shit. I'm drenched."

"I'll text them the coordinates. Start heading back this way," Troy said. "Luke, you're on."

I took a deep breath, filling my lungs and submerged. Luke climbed over the transom, gave a thumbs-up to Troy, and hopped into the water. He splashed below the surface and bubbles rose around him. He fiddled with his mask. It would take a moment for his eyes to adjust to the darkness. The Russian limpet mine was strapped around his chest.

I could hear the rumble of JD's motor through the water as he approached.

Luke angled towards the depths and kicked under the boat. It didn't take long for him to see me. I wasn't about to let him plant that mine. I launched toward him with my K-bar in my hand. I grabbed his mask, pulling it down. Without his visuals, he panicked. He didn't have any experience in underwater combat. I jammed the tip of the knife into his rib cage several times just below his armpit. Crimson blood oozed from the wound. It looked like black ink in the night.

With another quick slash, I severed his carotid artery. *So much for my less than lethal tactics.* I really didn't want to kill this person, but I couldn't compromise the mission. Instinct and training took over. I neutralized the threat. Nothing more, nothing less.

I grabbed the regulator and sucked in a breath of air. I pulled Luke's lifeless body down. He had enough negative buoyancy to sink. I took a last breath from the regulator and let Luke fall into the abyss, then I swam back to the surface by the stern of the ship.

About that time JD had arrived, and the *Slick'n Salty* was just about bow to bow with the *Heartbreaker*.

It was just about time to make my move.

35

They say if you don't like the weather in South Florida, just wait 45 minutes and it will change. Sure enough, the storm passed over, and the last sprinkles of rain settled.

"You got my stuff?" Troy shouted to JD as he stood on the foredeck.

"I got it," Jack said. "Let me see my daughter."

"It doesn't work that way. Show me the stuff, and I will show you the girl."

I climbed onto the swim platform and peered over the transom. Both Troy and Garrett were standing on the foredeck, negotiating with JD.

Jack opened the rolling suitcase and showed them the stash of fake cocaine.

I slipped over the transom and snuck into the deckhouse. I sheathed my K-bar and drew my 9mm, letting the water drain from the barrel. I left a trail of wet footprints across the deck as I moved past the galley.

Jack's boat was nice, but this *Valkyrie 63* was a behemoth. It was sleek and elegant with artful window lines, plush interior, every imaginable amenity, and spacious staterooms. It was part sport boat, part luxury yacht. The foredeck had a small lounge, and the bridge was accessible from the salon.

I pushed open the hatches of the staterooms and finally found Scarlett tied up in the master stateroom. With my K-bar, I cut the ropes around her wrists and ankles. Running mascara had stained her cheeks, and her eyes were puffy and red. I removed the gag from her mouth, and she wrapped her arms around me. "Thank God you're here!"

"Are you hurt?"

"No."

"I'm going to get you out of here. Don't worry."

"Where's Jack?"

"Distracting them."

I helped her off the bed and pulled her toward the hatch. I peered into the salon—it was empty. "Stay behind me. If things get ugly, get down and take cover."

The boat creaked and groaned as we tiptoed across the salon. I could see the foredeck through the forward windows. Garrett and Troy still negotiated with Jack. Their muffled voices filtered into the salon.

"Go get the girl and bring her forward," Troy said.

It was bad timing.

Garrett started aft.

Troy's girlfriend rounded the stern in a tender.

I flattened my back against the aft bulkhead. When Garrett pushed through the hatch, I chopped the side of my hand into his Adam's apple, crushing his trachea.

He wheezed for breath and clutched his throat.

A hard fist planted firmly in his stomach made him double over. Then a sharp elbow to his back flattened him on the deck. I dropped down and put him in a chokehold.

His face reddened, and his eyes bulged from their sockets. The hold cut off the blood flow to his brain, and within moments, Garrett passed out. His limp body flopped to the deck.

Troy's girlfriend saw me and shouted, alerting Troy. She pulled a pistol from her waistband and capped off several rounds. Muzzle flash flickered in the night.

I dove for cover behind the bulkhead.

Troy opened fire at JD with an AR-15. The muffled report of gunfire filtered into the deckhouse.

Scarlett shrieked in terror.

She hit the deck and crawled into the galley.

JD ran across the foredeck, returning fire. He dove into the water as Troy unleashed a torrent of bullets at the *Slick'n Salty*, peppering the fiberglass hull.

Troy continued firing into the water as JD submerged. He waited a few minutes for Jack to surface, but he never did.

I angled my weapon around the hatch and squeezed off two rounds. The sharp smell of gunpowder filled my nostrils.

Two bullets plunked into Troy's girlfriend—one in her chest, the other in her head.

Crimson blood blossomed on her shirt. She tumbled back, falling over the transom. Her body smacked the swim platform, then slipped into the water. She floated away, past the tender.

Troy backed away from the foredeck and ran aft. He screamed with grief, watching his girlfriend die before him. His face snarled with rage as he rounded the corner. A slew of bullets streaked in my direction. They snapped past my ears and drilled through the bulkheads.

In a combat situation, fine motor skills degrade. The rush of adrenaline and increased heart rate and blood pressure make things like aim deteriorate.

Troy was an amateur.

I was a professional.

According to law enforcement, most officer involved shootings occur within 10 feet, and 90% of shots miss. Combined with the rolling deck, and Troy's adrenaline, he missed every shot he took.

I double tapped him, just like I did his girlfriend. One in the chest, one in the head.

His body jerked and convulsed with each hit. Blood spewed from the entry wounds, and he crashed to the deck. His weapon clattered from his hand, discharging one final time as his finger inadvertently pulled the trigger.

Troy was dead, but his body still had a few random nerve

impulses left. He twitched for a few moments before his body finally settled.

The deck was awash with blood.

I checked myself for injuries. In the heightened state of battle, sometimes a gunshot wound can go unnoticed. It's not until after the adrenaline wears off that the pain sets in.

I felt my torso, legs, arms, and did a quick visual inspection.

No blood.

No bullet holes.

I holstered my weapon and moved forward to the galley.

Scarlett was balled up in the corner, trembling.

"It's okay. You're safe now."

I had no idea what condition JD was in.

I helped Scarlett to her feet, and we moved aft, toward the hatch. We stepped into the cockpit. Scarlett glared at Troy's lifeless body.

I didn't know if JD was alive or dead.

I heard something splashing in the water, and a moment later JD climbed onto the swim platform, then scaled the transom. His soaking wet clothes clung to his body. He breathed a sigh of relief when he saw Scarlett unharmed. The two ran into each other's arms and hugged each other tight.

"Are you okay?" Jack asked.

"I'm fine, Dad."

It was the first time she had called him *Dad* in a long time.

Those words were music to JD's ears. Jack held her in his arms like he never wanted to let go.

Maybe this is why I got a second chance—to bring a family back together? Maybe that was my purpose? And now that my destiny was fulfilled, would death be knocking at my door?

36

"What the hell are we going to do about this mess?" JD asked.

"I'll take care of it," I said. "Get her back on your boat."

Jack gave me a look of appreciation. "I owe you one, partner."

I smiled. "About rent on the boat..."

Jack grinned. "I wasn't going to make you pay it, anyway."

"What about my poker winnings?"

His eyes narrowed at me. "We'll discuss that."

I laughed.

Jack and Scarlett took Troy's tender back to the *Slick'n Salty*.

Troy's girlfriend's bloody body floating in the water had attracted the attention of several bull sharks. They were thrashing at the carcass in a frenzy. There wouldn't be much left of her when they were finished.

I moved back into the salon and checked Garrett's pulse. He was still alive. I found some rope and hogtied him.

I had a tough decision to make. Do I cover my tracks and pretend we were never here? Or do I call the sheriff?

Things could get sticky, and there might be a lot of questions. The old me would have killed Garrett, dumped the bodies, and set the boat on fire to cover my tracks.

But I didn't want to kill a man that wasn't an immediate threat. JD and I decided to call the sheriff. We waited for an hour for the water patrol to arrive.

The morning sun climbed over the horizon, painting the sky in vibrant colors.

At first I wasn't sure how Sheriff Daniels was going to react. But once I explained the situation, he seemed almost happy we had taken care of these cretins for him. Garrett made a full confession to the kidnapping and fingered Troy as Jeremy's and Dan's killer. They had been using Dan's boat for their smuggling operation. When Dan found out, he threatened to go to the police and tell them everything.

I made sure that Garrett knew he needed to come clean. Before the sheriff arrived, I told him that if he didn't confess, I'd feed him to the sharks.

I almost felt bad for him. I don't think he was a bad kid. He just got mixed up with the wrong crowd. Needed a little extra cash and made some poor decisions. He was just along for the ride when things spiraled out of control and Troy went full on psycho. Now he was going to spend the rest of his life behind bars.

By the time we were finished answering the Sheriff's questions, the sharks' feeding frenzy had dissipated. I retrieved the Dräger from the seafloor and boarded the *Slick'n Salty*. We swung around to the north side of Urchin Key and collected Jack's tender.

We made our way back to the marina, tied off, and reconnected water and power lines. Jack surveyed the damage to the boat. There were multiple bullet holes in the bow and foredeck. But all things considered, he got off cheap. It could have been much, much worse.

Scarlett gave me another hug and thanked me. "You're my hero, Tyson."

"What about me?" JD asked. "Don't I get any credit?"

Scarlett smiled and hugged him. "Maybe a little, Dad."

He helped her over the transom and onto the dock. She just wanted to get home, take a shower, and wash the terrible evening away.

I watched them walk down the dock, arm in arm. A little smile curled on my face. I moved into the deckhouse and grabbed a beer from the galley. I figured I deserved one after a night like that.

I climbed onto the bridge and enjoyed the morning, sipping my beer, letting the sun hit my face. I was thankful to be alive. At least for one more day.

I called Madison and let her know it was safe to come back. Then I texted Aria and let her know that I was back at the marina, and all was clear. I told her it had been a long night, and I was going to crawl into bed and get some sleep. She was more than welcome to stop by and join me at any time.

She replied: *Promise you won't shoot me if I sneak on board?*

As long as you behave, I texted.

I have no intention of behaving ;)

I smiled and crawled off to sleep in the master stateroom. I slept like a rock. The swim and the adrenaline rush had worn me out. When I crashed, I crashed hard. I barely heard the creak of the hatch when Aria slipped into the deck-house. I knew it was her from her soft footsteps.

As she snuck into my stateroom, I stretched and yawned and peeled an eye-open. By that time she was already undressing.

She had my full attention.

She crawled into bed and we embraced. "I missed you."

"I missed you, too."

We tumbled around for a while, then she snuggled up to me afterward. Man, she felt good in my arms.

I told her about our adventure, and she looked both terrified and intrigued.

The day was evaporating, and I was getting hungry. We both showered, got dressed, and made our way down the dock to *Diver Down*. Alejandro grilled us up some burgers, and by the time we finished, Madison had returned from South Beach.

I thought that she might be happy this was all over, but she was fuming. She had three days to stew in her own juices about being forced out of her home and place of business. I think if Aria hadn't been around Madison would've taken the gloves off.

I mustered my best, most charming smile and tried to talk Madison off the ledge. "I'm really sorry. I never meant to disrupt your life. The last thing I wanted was to get you involved in my mess. But everything is over now."

"It's over until the next time," Madison said.

"Hey, I had nothing to do with the guy who got murdered in your parking lot. You should be thanking me for bringing the killers to justice."

Madison sighed. "You're right. Thank you. I'm glad you got the guys who did it. But that doesn't mean you're off my shit list."

There was an awkward silence.

"So, are we all cool now?" I said, ignoring her last statement.

She rolled her eyes. "I think we're a long way from *cool*. But, I guess it's okay if you stick around for a while."

I smiled. "Good. I like being back home. I'm thinking about putting down roots."

Madison looked to Aria, "Honey, you're in for a wild ride."

She smiled. "I know."

My phone rang—*Unknown caller.*

"Excuse me, I gotta take this."

"Tyson..." Isabella said. "How did everything work out with your personal problem?"

"Good. Thanks for your help. It's all sorted."

"Excellent. It's time to return the favor. You ready for your next job?"

Ready for more?

The adventure continues with Wild Justice!

Join my newsletter and find out what happens next!

AUTHOR'S NOTE

Thanks for all the great reviews!

I've got more adventures for Tyson and JD. Stay tuned.

If you liked this book, let me know with a review on Amazon.

Thanks for reading!

—Tripp

TYSON WILD

Wild Ocean

Wild Justice

Wild Rivera

Wild Tide

Wild Rain

Wild Captive

Wild Killer

Wild Honor

Wild Gold

Wild Case

Wild Crown

Wild Break

Wild Fury

Wild Surge

Wild Impact

Wild...

MAX MARS

The Orion Conspiracy

Blade of Vengeance

The Zero Code

Edge of the Abyss

Siege on Star Cruise 239

Phantom Corps

The Auriga Incident

Devastator

CONNECT WITH ME

I'm just a geek who loves to write. Follow me on Facebook.

www.trippellis.com

Made in the USA
Las Vegas, NV
27 April 2023